Eze Bahii

ezekybahii@gmail.com

Osiris Code

The Awakening

Book One of the Osiris Code Series

Copyright © 2024 by Eze Bahii

Contents

2000 B.C.

Long, long ago, in a land called Egypt, there was a powerful pharaoh named Osiris. Osiris was kind and wise, and he loved his people very much. He ruled over the land with his beautiful wife, Isis, and their brave son, Horus.

Osiris was not just a great ruler; he was also very smart. He discovered a magical algorithm, a special code that could bring the dead back to life. This code was so powerful that it could change the world forever. Osiris called it the Osiris Code.

The Osiris Code was written in ancient symbols and hidden in a sacred scroll. Osiris kept the scroll in a special temple, guarded by magical creatures and powerful spells. Only the wisest and bravest could enter the temple and see the code.

Osiris knew that the Osiris Code was very important, so he kept it hidden and safe. He wanted to use it to help his people and make Egypt a better place. But Osiris had a brother named Set, who was very jealous of him. Set wanted to be the pharaoh and have all the power for himself.

One day, Set tricked Osiris and stole the Osiris Code. He hid the code in secret places all over Egypt, so no one could find it. Osiris was very sad and worried. He knew that if the wrong people found the code, they could use it for bad things.

Set was a cunning and evil man. He used dark magic to hide the pieces of the Osiris Code in ancient temples, hidden chambers, and even in the hearts of magical creatures. He wanted to make sure that no one could ever find the code and use it against him.

Isis and Horus were very upset when they found out what Set had done. They vowed to find the Osiris Code and restore Osiris to life. They knew it would be a hard and dangerous journey, but they were determined to do it.

Isis and Horus travelled all over Egypt, searching for the hidden pieces of the Osiris Code. They faced many challenges and dangers, but they never gave up. They knew that the future of Egypt depended on them.

They encountered magical guardians, ancient traps, and powerful spells. But Isis was very smart, and Horus was very brave. Together, they overcame every obstacle and found some of the hidden pieces of the code.

As they searched, Isis and Horus discovered that the Osiris Code was not just a magical algorithm; it was also connected to the gods and the ancient magic of Egypt. They learned that the code could bring back the dead, but it could also do much more. It could change the world in ways they never imagined.

They found some of the hidden pieces of the code, but they knew that there were still many more to find. They also knew that Set and his followers were looking for the code too, and they would do anything to get it.

Isis and Horus realized that the Osiris Code was not just a tool for resurrection; it was a key to understanding the secrets of life and death. They knew that if they could find all the pieces and restore Osiris to life, they could bring peace and prosperity to Egypt and the world.

Isis and Horus continued their journey, determined to find all the pieces of the Osiris Code and restore Osiris to life. They knew that the future of Egypt and the world depended on them.

And so, the search for the Osiris Code began, a search that would last for thousands of years and change the course of history forever. The legacy of Osiris, Isis, and

Horus would be remembered and honored by generations to come, as the quest for the Osiris Code continued.

Chapter 1: Present Day - Cairo, Egypt

Orenus's Daily Life

In the bustling city of Cairo, there lived a young boy named Orenus. Orenus was not like other kids his age. He loved computers and solving puzzles more than anything else. Every day, he would spend hours in front of his computer, exploring the internet and learning new things.

Orenus lived in a small apartment with his family. His parents worked hard to make sure he had everything he needed. They knew that Orenus was special and that he had a bright future ahead of him.

Every morning, Orenus would wake up early and get ready for school. He would put on his favorite t-shirt and jeans, grab his backpack, and head out the door. On his way to school, he would pass by the busy markets, the tall buildings, and the ancient pyramids that stood proudly in the distance.

At school, Orenus was known as the smart kid who loved computers. He would spend his free time in the computer lab, working on projects and helping his friends with their homework. His teachers were always impressed by his skills and encouraged him to keep learning.

After school, Orenus would rush home to continue his adventures on the computer. He would explore different websites, play games, and even try to hack into secret files. He loved the thrill of discovering new things and solving puzzles.

The Mysterious File

One day, after a long day at school, Orenus rushed home, eager to get back to his computer. He loved the feeling of discovering new things and solving puzzles. As he sat down at his desk, he turned on his computer and started browsing the internet.

Orenus had a special talent for finding hidden files and secret websites. He knew all the tricks and shortcuts to navigate the vast world of the internet. Today, he was feeling particularly adventurous. He decided to explore some of the darker corners of the web, where not many people dared to go.

As he clicked through various links and forums, he stumbled upon a strange website. The website had no name and no pictures, just a black background with a single link in the middle. The link was written in a language Orenus had never seen before. It was a mix of symbols and ancient Egyptian hieroglyphs.

Orenus's heart started to beat faster. He knew he had found something special. He clicked on the link, and a new page opened. The page was filled with more symbols and hieroglyphs, arranged in a pattern that looked like a code. Orenus was intrigued. He had always loved solving puzzles, and this one seemed like the biggest puzzle he had ever seen.

Orenus spent hours trying to decipher the symbols and hieroglyphs. He used all the tools and tricks he knew, but the code was unlike anything he had encountered before. He searched the internet for clues, looking for any information that could help him understand the mysterious file.

After a while, he found a website that talked about ancient Egyptian codes and symbols. The website explained that the hieroglyphs were used by the ancient Egyptians to write secret messages and spells. Orenus was fascinated. He started to compare the symbols on the mysterious file with the ones on the website.

Slowly, he began to make sense of the code. He realized that the symbols were arranged in a specific pattern, and each pattern had a meaning. He started to write down the meanings on a piece of paper, trying to piece together the message.

As he worked, Orenus felt a sense of excitement and wonder. He knew that he was uncovering something important, something that had been hidden for thousands of years. He couldn't wait to find out what it was.

After many hours of hard work, Orenus finally managed to decipher the entire code. He looked at the message he had written down and felt a shiver run down his spine. The message talked about a powerful algorithm called the Osiris Code, which could bring the dead back to life.

The message also mentioned a hidden temple in Cairo, where the first fragment of the Osiris Code was hidden. Orenus couldn't believe what he was reading. He had always loved stories about ancient Egypt and its magical secrets, but he never thought he would find something like this.

He knew that he had to find the hidden temple and the first fragment of the Osiris Code. He couldn't just sit back and do nothing. This was his chance to be part of something amazing, something that could change the world.

Orenus started to plan his next move. He knew that he would need to be careful and smart. The hidden temple was probably guarded by ancient traps and magical creatures. He would need to use all his skills and knowledge to navigate the temple and find the fragment.

He spent the rest of the night preparing for his adventure. He gathered all the tools and equipment he would need, including his laptop, a flashlight, and a map of Cairo. He also made sure to bring some snacks and water, just in case.

As he lay in bed that night, Orenus couldn't stop thinking about the Osiris Code and the hidden temple. He knew that the next day would be the start of an incredible journey, one that would change his life forever. He closed his eyes and tried to get some sleep, but his mind was racing with excitement and anticipation.

Deciphering the Clues

The next morning, Orenus woke up early, feeling a mix of excitement and nervousness. He knew that today was the day he would start his adventure to find the hidden temple and the first fragment of the Osiris Code. He quickly got dressed, grabbed his backpack filled with all the tools he needed, and headed out the door.

As he walked through the bustling streets of Cairo, Orenus couldn't help but feel a sense of wonder. He looked at the tall buildings, the ancient pyramids, and the busy markets, knowing that somewhere in this city lay a secret that had been hidden for thousands of years.

Orenus pulled out the map he had printed the night before. The map showed the location of the hidden temple, marked with a small red dot. He studied the map carefully, trying to figure out the best route to take. He knew that he would need to be careful and smart, as the temple was probably guarded by ancient traps and magical creatures.

Orenus started his journey, following the map through the winding streets of Cairo. He passed by ancient buildings and modern shops, feeling a sense of history and mystery all around him. As he walked, he kept his eyes open for any clues or signs that could help him find the temple.

After a while, Orenus reached a small, hidden alleyway. The alleyway was dark and narrow, but something about it felt right. He checked the map again and saw that the red dot was right in the middle of the alleyway. He took a deep breath and stepped inside.

The alleyway was filled with old, crumbling buildings and piles of rubble. Orenus carefully made his way through, looking for any signs of the hidden temple. He used his flashlight to light the way, shining it on the walls and the ground, searching for any clues.

Suddenly, he noticed a small, carved symbol on one of the walls. The symbol looked like one of the hieroglyphs from the mysterious file. Orenus's heart started to beat faster. He knew that he was on the right track.

Orenus studied the symbol carefully, trying to figure out what it meant. He remembered the patterns and meanings he had written down the night before and started to compare them with the symbol on the wall. Slowly, he began to decipher the clue.

The symbol pointed to a hidden door, concealed behind a pile of rubble. Orenus carefully moved the rubble aside, revealing a small, wooden door. The door was old and worn, but it was still locked tightly. Orenus knew that he would need to use his hacking skills to open it.

He pulled out his laptop and connected it to a small device he had brought with him. The device was a special tool that could hack into any lock, no matter how old or complicated it was. Orenus started to type in the codes and commands, feeling a sense of excitement and anticipation.

After a few minutes, the lock clicked open, and the door creaked slowly. Orenus pushed it open, revealing a dark, hidden chamber. He stepped inside, shining his flashlight around the room. The chamber was filled with ancient artifacts and strange symbols, all pointing to the hidden temple and the first fragment of the Osiris Code.

Orenus knew that he was one step closer to uncovering the secret of the Osiris Code. He took a deep breath and stepped further into the chamber, ready to face whatever challenges lay ahead.

The Journey Begins

Orenus stepped further into the hidden chamber, feeling a mix of excitement and nervousness. The chamber was dark and filled with ancient artifacts and strange symbols. He shone his flashlight around the room, taking in the mysterious surroundings.

The air was cool and damp, and the walls were covered in intricate carvings and hieroglyphs. Orenus could feel the weight of history all around him. He knew that he was standing in a place that had been hidden for thousands of years, a place that held the secrets of the Osiris Code.

He carefully made his way through the chamber, looking for any clues or signs that could help him find the first fragment of the code. He examined the artifacts and symbols, using his knowledge of ancient Egyptian culture and his hacking skills to decipher their meanings.

Suddenly, he noticed a small, glowing tablet resting on a pedestal in the center of the room. The tablet was covered in more hieroglyphs and symbols, and it seemed to be the source of the mysterious light that filled the chamber. Orenus approached the tablet cautiously, feeling a sense of awe and wonder.

As Orenus reached out to touch the tablet, he felt a surge of energy run through his body. The tablet glowed brighter, and the symbols on its surface began to move and change. Orenus watched in amazement as the symbols rearranged themselves, forming a new pattern that he recognized from the mysterious file.

He quickly pulled out his notebook and started to write down the pattern, feeling a sense of urgency and excitement. He knew that he had found the first fragment of the Osiris Code, and that this was just the beginning of his journey.

With the pattern safely recorded in his notebook, Orenus carefully placed the tablet back on the pedestal. He knew that he needed to leave the chamber and find a safe place to study the pattern and decipher its meaning. He also knew that he couldn't do this alone. He would need help from someone who understood the ancient magic and technology of Egypt.

As he made his way back through the chamber and out into the alleyway, Orenus felt a sense of determination and purpose. He knew that the journey ahead would be long and dangerous, but he was ready to face whatever challenges lay ahead. He had found the first fragment of the Osiris Code, and he was one step closer to uncovering its secrets.

With a final glance back at the hidden chamber, Orenus stepped out into the bustling streets of Cairo, ready to begin the next chapter of his adventure. He knew that he had a long way to go, but he was determined to see it through to the end. The journey had begun, and there was no turning back now.

Chapter 2: The Hidden Temple

Arrival at the Temple

Orenus walked through the bustling streets of Cairo, his heart pounding with excitement and a touch of fear. He clutched his backpack tightly, feeling the weight of the tools and equipment he had brought with him. The map he had printed the night before was folded neatly in his pocket, guiding him to the hidden temple.

The sun was high in the sky, casting a warm glow over the city. Orenus passed by ancient buildings and modern shops, feeling a sense of history and mystery all around him. He knew that he was on the brink of an incredible adventure, one that could change his life forever.

As he walked, Orenus kept his eyes open for any signs or clues that could help him find the temple. He studied the map carefully, making sure he was on the right path. The red dot marking the temple's location seemed to be getting closer with each step he took.

Finally, after what felt like hours, Orenus reached a small, hidden alleyway. The alleyway was dark and narrow, but something about it felt right. He checked the map again and saw that the red dot was right in the middle of the alleyway. He took a deep breath and stepped inside.

The alleyway was filled with old, crumbling buildings and piles of rubble. Orenus carefully made his way through, looking for any signs of the hidden temple. He used his flashlight to light the way, shining it on the walls and the ground, searching for any clues.

Suddenly, he noticed a small, carved symbol on one of the walls. The symbol looked like one of the hieroglyphs from the mysterious file. Orenus's heart started to beat faster. He knew that he was on the right track.

He studied the symbol carefully, trying to figure out what it meant. He remembered the patterns and meanings he had written down the night before and started to compare them with the symbol on the wall. Slowly, he began to decipher the clue.

The symbol pointed to a hidden door, concealed behind a pile of rubble. Orenus carefully moved the rubble aside, revealing a small, wooden door. The door was old and worn, but it was still locked tightly. Orenus knew that he would need to use his hacking skills to open it.

He pulled out his laptop and connected it to a small device he had brought with him. The device was a special tool that could hack into any lock, no matter how old or complicated it was. Orenus started to type in the codes and commands, feeling a sense of excitement and anticipation.

After a few minutes, the lock clicked open, and the door creaked slowly. Orenus pushed it open, revealing a dark, hidden chamber. He stepped inside, shining his flashlight around the room. The chamber was filled with ancient artifacts and strange symbols, all pointing to the hidden temple and the first fragment of the Osiris Code.

Orenus took a deep breath and stepped further into the chamber, ready to face whatever challenges lay ahead. He knew that he was one step closer to uncovering the secret of the Osiris Code. The journey had begun, and there was no turning back now.

Exploring the Temple

Orenus stepped further into the hidden chamber, his flashlight casting eerie shadows on the ancient walls. The air was cool and damp, filled with the scent of old stone and dust. He could feel the weight of history all around him, as if the chamber itself was whispering secrets from the past.

The chamber was vast, with high ceilings and intricate carvings covering every surface. Orenus shone his flashlight around, taking in the mysterious surroundings. He saw statues of ancient Egyptian gods, their eyes seeming to follow him as he moved. There were also piles of old artifacts, covered in dust and cobwebs, waiting to be discovered.

Orenus started to explore the chamber, his heart pounding with excitement and a touch of fear. He knew that he was standing in a place that had been hidden for thousands of years, a place that held the secrets of the Osiris Code. He had to be careful and smart, as the temple was probably guarded by ancient traps and magical creatures.

As he walked, Orenus noticed that the floor was covered in strange symbols and patterns. He recognized some of the hieroglyphs from the mysterious file and knew that they were part of the code. He started to take pictures of the symbols with his phone, making sure to capture every detail.

Suddenly, he heard a faint noise coming from deeper within the temple. It sounded like the rustling of wings or the whispering of voices. Orenus froze, his heart racing. He knew that he wasn't alone in the temple. There was something else here, something ancient and powerful.

Orenus took a deep breath and continued to explore the temple, his senses on high alert. He knew that he had to be brave and face whatever challenges lay ahead. He had come this far, and he wasn't going to turn back now.

As he moved deeper into the temple, Orenus discovered more chambers and hidden passages. Each one was filled with more artifacts and symbols, all pointing to the Osiris Code. He took more pictures and made notes in his notebook, feeling a sense of awe and wonder at the ancient secrets he was uncovering.

In one of the chambers, Orenus found a large stone tablet covered in hieroglyphs. The tablet was surrounded by statues of ancient Egyptian gods, their eyes seeming to watch him as he approached. He knew that this tablet was important, that it held a key piece of the Osiris Code.

He started to decipher the hieroglyphs, using his knowledge of ancient Egyptian culture and his hacking skills. Slowly, he began to make sense of the symbols and their meanings. He realized that the tablet was a map, showing the location of the next fragment of the Osiris Code.

Just as he was about to take a picture of the tablet, Orenus heard the noise again. This time, it was louder and closer. He turned around quickly, his flashlight shining into the darkness. He saw a shadow moving in the distance, a shadow that seemed to be coming towards him.

Orenus's heart was pounding in his chest as he backed away from the shadow, his flashlight shaking in his hand. He knew that he had to be careful and smart, that he couldn't let fear take over. He had to face whatever was coming towards him and find a way to overcome it.

As the shadow came closer, Orenus saw that it was a large, winged creature. The creature had the body of a lion and the head of a hawk, its eyes glowing in the darkness. Orenus recognized it from the ancient Egyptian myths he had read about. It was a sphinx, a magical guardian of the temple.

The sphinx stopped in front of Orenus, its eyes fixed on him. Orenus knew that he had to act quickly, that he had to find a way to communicate with the creature and convince it that he meant no harm. He remembered the stories he had read about sphinxes, about how they loved riddles and puzzles.

"I come in peace," Orenus said, his voice shaking slightly. "I am here to uncover the secrets of the Osiris Code, to help bring balance to the world. I mean no harm to you or the temple."

The sphinx tilted its head, its eyes narrowing as it studied Orenus. "You seek the Osiris Code," it said, its voice like thunder. "But you must prove yourself worthy. Answer my riddle, and I will let you pass. Fail, and you will face my wrath."

Orenus took a deep breath, his mind racing as he prepared to face the sphinx's challenge. He knew that this was a test, a test of his wits and his courage. He was ready to face it head-on.

The Hidden Chamber

Orenus stood before the sphinx, his heart pounding in his chest. He knew that he had to answer the sphinx's riddle correctly to prove himself worthy and gain access to the hidden chamber. He took a deep breath and focused his mind, ready to face the challenge.

"What walks on four legs in the morning, two legs at noon, and three legs in the evening?" the sphinx asked, its voice echoing through the chamber.

Orenus thought carefully, his mind racing through the possibilities. He remembered the stories he had read about sphinxes and their riddles. He knew that the answer had to be something that changed over time, something that could be interpreted in different ways.

Suddenly, it clicked. "A human," Orenus said confidently. "A human crawls on four legs as a baby, walks on two legs as an adult, and uses a cane, which is like a third leg, in old age."

The sphinx nodded, its eyes glowing with approval. "You have answered correctly," it said. "You may pass."

With a sense of relief and triumph, Orenus stepped past the sphinx and continued deeper into the temple. He knew that he was one step closer to uncovering the secrets of the Osiris Code.

As he walked, Orenus noticed that the walls of the temple were covered in more intricate carvings and hieroglyphs. He recognized some of the symbols from the mysterious file and knew that they were part of the code. He started to take pictures of the symbols with his phone, making sure to capture every detail.

Suddenly, he came across a hidden door, concealed behind a large statue of the god Anubis. The door was small and unassuming, but Orenus knew that it led to something important. He approached the door cautiously, his heart racing with anticipation.

Orenus studied the door carefully, looking for any clues or signs that could help him open it. He noticed that the door was covered in more hieroglyphs, arranged in a specific pattern. He recognized the pattern from the mysterious file and knew that it was a code that needed to be deciphered.

He pulled out his notebook and started to write down the hieroglyphs, comparing them with the patterns and meanings he had recorded earlier. Slowly, he began to decipher the code. He realized that the hieroglyphs formed a sequence that had to be entered in a specific order to open the door.

Orenus took a deep breath and started to enter the sequence on a small keypad hidden in the wall next to the door. He pressed each button carefully, making sure to follow the exact order of the hieroglyphs. After a few tense moments, the door clicked open, revealing a dark, hidden chamber.

Orenus stepped inside, his flashlight shining around the room. The chamber was small and filled with ancient artifacts and strange symbols. He could feel the weight of history all around him, as if the chamber itself was whispering secrets from the past.

In the center of the chamber, Orenus saw a small, glowing tablet resting on a pedestal. The tablet was covered in more hieroglyphs and symbols, and it seemed to be the source of the mysterious light that filled the chamber. Orenus approached the tablet cautiously, feeling a sense of awe and wonder.

As Orenus reached out to touch the tablet, he felt a surge of energy run through his body. The tablet glowed brighter, and the symbols on its surface began to move and change. Orenus watched in amazement as the symbols rearranged themselves, forming a new pattern that he recognized from the mysterious file.

He quickly pulled out his notebook and started to write down the pattern, feeling a sense of urgency and excitement. He knew that he had found the first fragment of the Osiris Code, and that this was just the beginning of his journey.

With the pattern safely recorded in his notebook, Orenus carefully placed the tablet back on the pedestal. He knew that he needed to leave the chamber and find a safe place to study the pattern and decipher its meaning. He also knew that he couldn't do this alone. He would need help from someone who understood the ancient magic and technology of Egypt.

As he made his way back through the chamber and out into the temple, Orenus felt a sense of determination and purpose. He knew that the journey ahead would be long and dangerous, but he was ready to face whatever challenges lay ahead. He had found the first fragment of the Osiris Code, and he was one step closer to uncovering its secrets.

Suddenly, Orenus heard a noise coming from deeper within the temple. It sounded like footsteps, and they were getting closer. He froze, his heart racing. He knew that he wasn't alone in the temple. There was someone else here, someone who might be after the Osiris Code as well.

Orenus quickly hid behind a large statue, his flashlight turned off. He peeked out from behind the statue, trying to see who was coming. He saw a figure emerging from the darkness, a figure that seemed to be searching for something.

The figure was dressed in dark clothes and carried a small device in their hand. Orenus recognized the device as a high-tech scanner, something that could be used to detect hidden artifacts and symbols. He knew that this person was not here by accident. They were looking for the Osiris Code, just like he was.

Orenus watched as the figure moved through the temple, scanning the walls and artifacts with the device. He knew that he had to be careful and smart. He couldn't let this person find the Osiris Code before he did. He had to find a way to outsmart them and protect the code at all costs.

As the figure came closer, Orenus saw that it was a woman. She had long, dark hair and piercing eyes that seemed to see right through him. She moved with a sense of purpose and determination, as if she knew exactly what she was looking for.

The First Fragment

Orenus stepped out from behind the statue, his heart pounding in his chest. He knew that he had to act quickly and decisively. The woman with the scanner was getting closer, and he couldn't let her find the first fragment of the Osiris Code before he did.

He took a deep breath and called out to the woman, "Who are you, and what are you doing here?"

The woman turned to face Orenus, her piercing eyes studying him carefully. "I could ask you the same question," she replied, her voice calm and steady. "But I think we both know why we're here. We're looking for the Osiris Code."

Orenus felt a mix of fear and determination. He knew that he had to be smart and careful. He couldn't let this woman take the fragment from him. "I found it first," he said firmly. "And I'm not going to let you take it."

The woman smiled slightly, her eyes glinting in the dim light of the temple. "I see," she said. "Well, perhaps we can work together. My name is Alledas, and I'm a member of the Seekers. We're a secret society dedicated to protecting the balance between magic and technology.

We've been searching for the Osiris Code for a very long time."

Orenus hesitated, unsure of whether he could trust this woman. But he knew that he needed help, and the Seekers sounded like they might be the right people to help him. "I'm Orenus," he said cautiously. "And I found the first fragment of the Osiris Code. But I don't know what to do with it."

Alledas nodded, her expression serious. "The Osiris Code is very powerful and very dangerous," she said. "It can bring the dead back to life, but it can also do much more. It's connected to the ancient magic of Egypt, and it's been hidden for thousands of years for a reason."

Orenus felt a shiver run down his spine. He knew that he had found something important, something that could change the world. "So what do we do now?" he asked.

Alledas looked around the temple, her eyes scanning the ancient artifacts and symbols. "We need to get the fragment to a safe place," she said. "The Seekers have a headquarters hidden beneath the city. We can study the fragment there and figure out what to do next."

Orenus nodded, feeling a sense of relief and excitement. He knew that he had found an ally, someone who could help him on his journey. "Okay," he said. "Let's go."

Together, Orenus and Alledas made their way back through the temple, careful to avoid any traps or guardians. They moved quickly and quietly, their senses on high alert. As they reached the entrance of the temple, Orenus took one last look back at the ancient chamber, feeling a sense of awe and wonder at the secrets it held.

With Alledas by his side, he felt a new sense of confidence and determination. They had the first fragment of the Osiris Code, and they were one step closer to uncovering its secrets.

As they stepped out into the bustling streets of Cairo, Orenus couldn't help but feel a sense of excitement and anticipation.

Chapter 3: The Seekers' Headquarters

Arrival at the Headquarters

Orenus followed Alledas through the winding streets of Cairo, his heart pounding with excitement and a touch of nervousness. He knew that he was about to enter a world of ancient secrets and powerful magic, a world that had been hidden for thousands of years.

Finally, they reached a small, hidden doorway in the heart of the city. The doorway was concealed behind a pile of rubble, and it was guarded by ancient symbols and magical wards. Alledas approached the doorway and whispered a secret password. The symbols on the door glowed briefly, and then the door creaked open, revealing a dark, hidden passage.

Orenus took a deep breath and stepped inside, following Alledas down a long, winding staircase. The air was cool and damp, filled with the scent of old stone and dust. He could feel the weight of history all around him, as if the passage itself was whispering secrets from the past.

As they descended deeper into the passage, Orenus noticed that the walls were lined with ancient artifacts and symbols. He recognized some of the hieroglyphs from the mysterious file and knew that they were part of the Osiris Code. He started to take pictures of the symbols with his phone, making sure to capture every detail.

Finally, after what felt like an eternity, they reached the bottom of the staircase. Alledas led Orenus through a large, arched doorway, and they stepped into a vast, underground chamber. The chamber was filled with ancient artifacts and strange symbols, all pointing to the secrets of the Osiris Code.

Orenus looked around the chamber in awe, taking in the mysterious surroundings. The walls were lined with maps, scrolls, and ancient texts, all arranged in a way that seemed both chaotic and orderly at the same time. In the center of the room stood a large, round table, surrounded by chairs carved from ancient wood.

As they stepped further into the chamber, Orenus noticed that there were other people in the room, all dressed in dark robes and carrying ancient artifacts. They were the other members of the Seekers, and they welcomed Orenus with open arms.

Alledas introduced Orenus to the other members, explaining his role in finding the first fragment of the Osiris Code and his decision to join the Seekers. The other members nodded in approval, their eyes filled with respect and admiration.

"Welcome to the Seekers, Orenus," said one of the members, a tall man with piercing eyes. "We are honored to have you join us on this important mission."

Orenus felt a sense of belonging and purpose.

Suddenly, a young woman with short, curly hair and bright eyes approached Orenus. She was dressed in a dark robe, but she also wore a small device on her wrist that looked like a high-tech watch.

"Hi, I'm Vohowa," she said, extending her hand. "I'm the tech expert around here. I heard you're pretty good with computers too."

Orenus smiled, feeling a sense of camaraderie. "Yeah, I love computers and solving puzzles," he said. "It's nice to meet you, Vohowa."

Vohowa grinned, her eyes sparkling with excitement. "I can't wait to show you all the cool tech we have here," she said. "We're going to have so much fun working together."

Orenus felt a sense of excitement and anticipation. He knew that he was standing on the brink of an incredible adventure, one that would change his life forever.

Introduction to the Seekers

Orenus followed Alledas and Vohowa deeper into the Seekers' headquarters, his eyes wide with wonder. The vast underground chamber was filled with ancient artifacts and strange symbols, all pointing to the secrets of the Osiris Code. He could feel the weight of history all around him, as if the chamber itself was whispering secrets from the past.

Alledas led Orenus to a large, circular room filled with maps, scrolls, and ancient texts. In the center of the room stood a large, round table, surrounded by chairs carved from ancient wood. Orenus recognized the room as the mission room, where the Seekers planned their missions and discussed their findings.

"This is our mission room," Alledas explained. "It is where we plan our missions and discuss our findings. It is the heart of the Seekers' operations."

Orenus looked around the room in awe, taking in the ancient artifacts and the sense of purpose that filled the air. He knew that he was standing in a place of great importance, a place where the fate of the world was decided.

Alledas gestured for Orenus to take a seat at the table. She sat down opposite him, her eyes filled with determination. "The Seekers have been around for centuries," she began. "Our mission is to guard the balance between magic and technology. We believe that the ancient secrets of Egypt hold the key to understanding the true nature of the world and the power that lies within it."

"The Seekers were founded by a group of wise and brave individuals who dedicated their lives to protecting the ancient secrets of Egypt," Alledas continued. "They used their knowledge of ancient magic and advanced technology to navigate the hidden temples and uncover the secrets of the Osiris Code."

Orenus listened intently, his mind racing with excitement and curiosity. He knew that he was standing on the brink of an incredible adventure, one that could change the course of history.

"Over the centuries, the Seekers have found many fragments of the Osiris Code," Alledas said. "But there are still many more to find, and the journey is long and dangerous. We use a combination of ancient magic and advanced technology to overcome any obstacle and achieve our mission."

Vohowa, the tech expert, stepped forward and placed a small device on the table. The device looked like a high-tech tablet, but it was covered in ancient symbols and hieroglyphs. "This is one of our most advanced tools," she explained. "It combines ancient magic and modern technology, allowing us to decipher the Osiris Code and navigate the hidden temples."

Orenus picked up the device, his eyes widening as he examined the intricate symbols and advanced technology. He could feel the power of the device in his hands, as if it was whispering secrets from the past.

"The Seekers have access to ancient texts and artifacts, as well as the latest technological tools and devices," Alledas said. "Together, we can overcome any obstacle and achieve our mission."

"And now, with your help, we are one step closer to finding the Osiris Code," Alledas said, her voice filled with pride and determination. "The tablet you found is the first fragment, and it will help us unlock the secrets of the code. But there are still many more fragments to find, and the journey will be long and dangerous."

Orenus felt a sense of purpose and determination.

"The Seekers use a combination of ancient magic and advanced technology to navigate the hidden temples and uncover the secrets of the Osiris Code," Alledas explained. "We have access to ancient texts and artifacts, as well as the latest technological tools and devices. Together, we can overcome any obstacle and achieve our mission."

Vohowa grinned, her eyes sparkling with excitement. "I can't wait to show you all the cool tech we have here," she said. "We're going to have so much fun working together."

Orenus looked around the room, taking in the ancient artifacts and the sense of purpose that filled the air. He knew that he was standing in a place of great importance, a place where the fate of the world was decided. He was ready to be a part of it, to join the Seekers on their mission and help protect the Osiris Code.

Training with the Seekers

Orenus woke up early the next morning, feeling a mix of excitement and nervousness. He knew that today was the day he would begin his training with the Seekers. He quickly got dressed and headed to the mission room, where Alledas and Vohowa were waiting for him.

"Good morning, Orenus," Alledas said, her voice warm and welcoming. "Today, we will begin your training. You will learn about ancient magic and advanced technology, and how to use them to navigate the hidden temples and uncover the secrets of the Osiris Code."

Orenus nodded, his heart pounding with anticipation. He knew that he was standing on the brink of an incredible adventure, one that would change his life forever.

Alledas led Orenus to a large, open room filled with ancient artifacts and strange symbols. The room was lined with maps, scrolls, and ancient texts, all arranged in a way that seemed both chaotic and orderly at the same time. In the center of the room stood a large, round table, surrounded by chairs carved from ancient wood.

"This is our training room," Alledas explained. "It is where we practice our skills and abilities, where we learn to combine ancient magic and advanced technology to achieve our mission."

Vohowa stepped forward, her eyes sparkling with excitement. "I can't wait to show you all the cool tech we have here," she said. "We're going to have so much fun working together."

Vohowa led Orenus to a large, high-tech device that looked like a combination of a computer and an ancient artifact. The device was covered in intricate symbols and advanced technology, and it glowed with a mysterious light.

"This is one of our most advanced tools," Vohowa explained. "It combines ancient magic and modern technology, allowing us to decipher the Osiris Code and navigate the hidden temples. Today, you will learn how to use it."

Orenus approached the device, his eyes widening as he examined the intricate symbols and advanced technology. He could feel the power of the device in his hands, as if it was whispering secrets from the past.

Vohowa showed Orenus how to operate the device, explaining the different functions and features. She demonstrated how to enter the hieroglyphs and symbols from the Osiris Code, how to decipher their meanings, and how to use the device to navigate the hidden temples.

Orenus listened intently, his mind racing with excitement and curiosity. He knew that he was standing on the brink of an incredible adventure, one that could change the course of history.

After a few hours of practice, Orenus started to feel more confident in his abilities. He could operate the device with ease, entering the hieroglyphs and symbols from the Osiris Code and deciphering their meanings. He knew that he was one step closer to uncovering the secrets of the code.

As the day wore on, Orenus continued his training with the Seekers. He learned about the ancient magic used by the Seekers, about the spells and rituals that could be used to navigate the hidden temples and uncover the secrets of the Osiris Code.

Alledas showed Orenus how to cast simple spells, how to use ancient artifacts to enhance his abilities, and how to combine ancient magic and advanced technology to achieve his mission. She explained the importance of balance, of using magic and technology in harmony to achieve the best results.

Orenus practiced his new skills and abilities, feeling a sense of awe and wonder at the power of ancient magic and advanced technology. He knew that he was standing on the brink of an incredible adventure, one that could change the course of history.

As the day came to an end, Orenus felt a sense of pride and accomplishment. He knew that he had made great progress in his training, that he was one step closer to uncovering the secrets of the Osiris Code.

Alledas and Vohowa congratulated Orenus on his progress, their eyes filled with pride and respect. "You have done well today, Orenus," Alledas said. "You are a natural, and you have the potential to achieve great things. Together, we will uncover the secrets of the Osiris Code and bring balance to the world."

Orenus smiled, his heart filled with determination and excitement.

Understanding the Tablet

After a long day of training, Orenus felt both exhausted and exhilarated. He had learned so much about ancient magic and advanced technology, and he was eager to put his new skills to use. Alledas and Vohowa led him back to the mission room, where the glowing tablet with the first fragment of the Osiris Code was waiting.

Vohowa sat down at the large, round table and placed the tablet in front of her. She looked at Orenus with a serious expression. "This tablet is incredibly important," she said. "It holds the first fragment of the Osiris Code, and it's our key to unlocking the secrets of the code."

Orenus nodded, his eyes fixed on the glowing tablet. He could feel the power emanating from it, as if it was whispering ancient secrets. "What do we need to do next?" he asked, his voice filled with determination.

Vohowa pulled out a high-tech scanner and started to examine the tablet. She explained each symbol and hieroglyph, deciphering their meanings and explaining their significance. "The Osiris Code is not just a magical algorithm," she said. "It's a combination of ancient magic and advanced technology. It holds the power of resurrection, but it also has the potential to change the world in ways we can't even imagine."

Orenus listened intently, his mind racing with excitement and curiosity. He knew that the Osiris Code was too powerful to be left unprotected, that it had to be guarded and used for good.

"The danger lies in the hands of those who would use the Osiris Code for their own gain," Vohowa continued. "If the wrong people get their hands on the code, they could use it to control life and death itself. They could use it to gain ultimate power and rule the world."

Orenus felt a shiver run down his spine. He knew that the stakes were high, that the mission of the Seekers was of utmost importance. He was determined to help protect the Osiris Code and ensure it was used for good.

"But with your help, Orenus, we can make sure that doesn't happen," Vohowa said, her voice filled with confidence. "Together, we can uncover the secrets of the Osiris Code and use it to bring balance to the world."

Orenus nodded, his heart filled with determination. "I'm ready to do whatever it takes," he said. "I want to help protect the Osiris Code and make sure it doesn't fall into the wrong hands."

Vohowa smiled, her eyes filled with pride and respect. "I'm glad to hear that," she said. "Together, we can achieve great things. We can uncover the secrets of the Osiris Code and ensure that it is used for good."

As they continued to discuss the importance of the Osiris Code and the dangers it posed, Orenus felt a sense of purpose and determination.

With the first fragment of the Osiris Code safely in their possession, Orenus and Vohowa knew that the journey had just begun. There were still many more fragments to find, and the road ahead would be filled with danger and excitement. But they were determined to see it through to the end, to protect the Osiris Code and bring balance to the world.

Chapter 4: The Rival Organization

The Ankh Society

The next morning, Orenus woke up feeling refreshed and ready for whatever challenges the day might bring. He had spent the previous day training with the Seekers, learning about ancient magic and advanced technology, and he was eager to put his new skills to use.

As he made his way to the mission room, he found Alledas and Vohowa already there, deep in conversation. They looked up as he entered, their expressions serious.

"Good morning, Orenus," Alledas said, her voice filled with concern. "We have something important to discuss with you."

Orenus took a seat at the large, round table, his heart pounding with anticipation. He knew that whatever they were about to tell him was serious.

"We have received some troubling news," Alledas began. "There is a rival tech corporation called the Ankh Society. They are also after the Osiris Code, and they will stop at nothing to get their hands on it."

Orenus felt a shiver run down his spine. He knew that the Osiris Code was too powerful to be left unprotected, that it had to be guarded and used for good. The thought of a rival organization trying to steal it was terrifying.

"The Ankh Society is a powerful and ruthless corporation," Alledas continued. "They have access to advanced technology and are willing to use any means necessary to achieve their goals. They believe that the Osiris Code will give them ultimate power and control over the world."

Vohowa pulled out a high-tech tablet and showed Orenus a series of images and documents. "These are some of the Ankh Society's recent activities," she explained. "They have been conducting secret experiments and gathering information about the Osiris Code. They are getting closer to finding the remaining fragments, and we need to stop them."

Orenus looked at the images and documents, his eyes widening in shock. He saw pictures of high-tech labs, ancient artifacts, and even some familiar symbols from the Osiris Code. He knew that the Ankh Society was a serious threat, and that the Seekers had to act quickly to protect the code.

"What can we do to stop them?" Orenus asked, his voice filled with determination.

Alledas looked at Orenus, her eyes filled with pride and respect. "We need to be one step ahead of them at all times," she said. "We need to find the remaining fragments of the Osiris Code before they do, and we need to protect the code at all costs."

Vohowa nodded in agreement. "We have a plan," she said. "We will use our advanced technology and ancient magic to stay ahead of the Ankh Society. We will gather information, decipher the code, and navigate the hidden temples before they can."

Orenus felt a sense of purpose and determination.

"I'm ready to do whatever it takes," Orenus said, his voice filled with resolve. "Together, we can protect the Osiris Code and make sure it doesn't fall into the wrong hands."

Alledas and Vohowa smiled, their eyes filled with pride and respect. Alledas said. "We will uncover the secrets of the Osiris Code and bring balance to the world."

The Threat

Orenus sat at the large, round table in the mission room, his mind racing with the new information about the Ankh Society. He knew that the threat was real and that the Seekers had to act quickly to protect the Osiris Code.

Alledas stood up and walked to a large map on the wall. The map showed various locations around the world, marked with symbols and notes. "The Ankh Society has been conducting their operations in secret," she explained. "They have labs and facilities hidden in different parts of the world, all dedicated to finding and using the Osiris Code for their own gain."

Vohowa pulled out a high-tech tablet and showed Orenus more images and documents. "These are some of their recent activities," she said. "They have been experimenting with ancient artifacts and advanced technology, trying to decipher the Osiris Code. They are getting dangerously close to finding the remaining fragments."

Orenus looked at the images and documents, his heart pounding with concern. He saw pictures of high-tech labs filled with strange machines and ancient artifacts. He knew that the Ankh Society was a serious threat, and that the Seekers had to act quickly to protect the code.

"The Ankh Society believes that the Osiris Code will give them ultimate power," Alledas continued. "They want to use it to control life and death, to gain dominion over the world. If they succeed, the consequences could be catastrophic."

Orenus felt a shiver run down his spine. He knew that the stakes were high, that the mission of the Seekers was of utmost importance. He was determined to help protect the Osiris Code and ensure it was used for good.

"We need to be prepared for anything," Alledas said, her voice filled with determination. "The Ankh Society will stop at nothing to get their hands on the Osiris Code. They have powerful technology and are willing to use any means necessary to achieve their goals."

Vohowa nodded in agreement. "We need to stay one step ahead of them at all times," she said. "We need to gather information, decipher the code, and navigate the hidden temples before they can. We need to protect the Osiris Code at all costs."

Orenus looked around the room, taking in the ancient artifacts and the sense of purpose that filled the air. He knew that he was standing in a place of great importance, a place where the fate of the world was decided.

"What can we do to stop them?" Orenus asked, his voice filled with resolve.

Alledas looked at Orenus, her eyes filled with pride and respect. "We need to be smart and strategic," she said. "We need to use our advanced technology and ancient magic to stay ahead of the Ankh Society. We need to find the remaining fragments of the Osiris Code before they do, and we need to protect the code at all costs."

Vohowa pulled out a high-tech device and showed Orenus a series of maps and plans. "These are our strategies for staying ahead of the Ankh Society," she explained. "We will use our advanced technology to gather information and track their movements. We will use our ancient magic to navigate the hidden temples and uncover the secrets of the Osiris Code."

Orenus listened intently, his mind racing with excitement and curiosity. He knew that the Seekers had a plan, that they were prepared to face the threat posed by the Ankh Society. He was ready to do whatever it took to protect the Osiris Code and ensure it was used for good.

"We will also need to be prepared for confrontations," Alledas said, her voice serious. "The Ankh Society will not give up easily. They will try to steal the Osiris Code by any means necessary. We need to be ready to defend ourselves and the code at all costs."

First Encounter

The next day, Orenus, Alledas, and Vohowa were in the mission room, discussing their plans to stay ahead of the Ankh Society. The room was filled with maps, scrolls, and ancient texts, all arranged in a way that seemed both chaotic and orderly at the same time. The air was thick with tension and anticipation.

Suddenly, an alarm blared through the headquarters, echoing off the ancient stone walls. Alledas jumped to her feet, her eyes wide with concern. "That's the security alarm," she said, her voice filled with urgency. "Someone has breached our defenses."

Vohowa quickly pulled out her high-tech tablet and started scanning the security feeds. "It's the Ankh Society," she said, her voice shaking slightly. "They're here, and they're after the tablet."

Orenus felt a surge of adrenaline rush through his body. He knew that this was the moment they had been preparing for, the moment when they would face the Ankh Society for the first time. He was ready to do whatever it took to protect the Osiris Code.

Alledas turned to Orenus and Vohowa, her eyes filled with determination. "We need to act quickly," she said. "We need to protect the tablet and make sure it doesn't fall into the wrong hands."

Vohowa nodded, her eyes sparkling with excitement and fear. "I have a plan," she said. "We can use our advanced technology and ancient magic to create a diversion and escape with the tablet."

Orenus felt a sense of purpose and determination.

Alledas, Vohowa, and Orenus quickly gathered their equipment and made their way to the entrance of the headquarters. They could hear the sound of footsteps and voices echoing through the ancient stone corridors, growing louder and closer with each passing moment.

As they reached the entrance, they saw a group of men and women dressed in dark suits and carrying high-tech weapons. They were the members of the Ankh Society, and they were determined to get their hands on the Osiris Code.

Alledas stepped forward, her voice filled with authority. "You are trespassing on sacred ground," she said. "Leave now, or face the consequences."

The leader of the Ankh Society, a tall man with cold, calculating eyes, stepped forward. "We are here for the Osiris Code," he said. "Hand it over, and no one will get hurt."

Orenus felt a shiver run down his spine. He knew that the Ankh Society was a serious threat, and that the Seekers had to act quickly to protect the code. He was ready to do whatever it took to help the Seekers escape with the tablet.

Vohowa pulled out a small device from her pocket and activated it. The device emitted a bright, blinding light, filling the corridor with a dazzling display of colors and shapes. The members of the Ankh Society were momentarily disoriented, giving the Seekers the chance they needed to escape.

Alledas, Vohowa, and Orenus quickly made their way through the corridors, using their knowledge of the ancient magic and advanced technology to navigate the hidden passages and secret doors. They could hear the sound of footsteps and voices behind them, growing louder and closer with each passing moment.

As they reached a large, open chamber filled with ancient artifacts and strange symbols, Alledas turned to Orenus and Vohowa. "We need to split up," she said. "It will be harder for them to track us if we go in different directions."

Vohowa nodded, her eyes filled with determination. "I'll take the tablet and head to the secret exit," she said. "You two create a diversion and lead them away from me."

Alledas and Orenus quickly made their way through the chamber, using their advanced technology and ancient magic to create a diversion and lead the Ankh Society away from Vohowa. They activated ancient traps and magical wards, filling the chamber with a dazzling display of lights and sounds.

The members of the Ankh Society were momentarily disoriented, giving Alledas and Orenus the chance they needed to escape. They quickly made their way through the corridors, using their knowledge of the ancient magic and advanced technology to navigate the hidden passages and secret doors.

As they reached the entrance of the headquarters, they saw that the members of the Ankh Society were still in pursuit. Alledas turned to Orenus, her eyes filled with determination. "We need to create another diversion," she said. "We need to lead them away from Vohowa and the tablet."

Orenus nodded, his heart pounding with excitement and fear. He knew that this was the moment they had been preparing for, the moment when they would face the Ankh Society for the first time.

Alledas and Orenus quickly made their way through the streets of Cairo, using their knowledge of the ancient magic and advanced technology to create a diversion and lead the Ankh Society away from Vohowa and the tablet. They activated ancient traps and magical wards, filling the streets with a dazzling display of lights and sounds.

The members of the Ankh Society were momentarily disoriented, giving Alledas and Orenus the chance they needed to escape. They quickly made their way through the winding streets of Cairo, using their knowledge of the ancient magic and advanced technology to navigate the hidden passages and secret doors.

As they reached a safe location, Alledas turned to Orenus, her eyes filled with pride and respect. "You have done well today, Orenus," she said.

Planning the Next Move

After the intense encounter with the Ankh Society, Orenus, Alledas, and Vohowa regrouped in a safe location hidden within the bustling streets of Cairo. The adrenaline from their escape was still coursing through their veins, but they knew they had to stay focused and plan their next move.

Alledas looked at Orenus and Vohowa with a serious expression. "We need to stay one step ahead of the Ankh Society," she said. "They will not give up easily, and they will be even more determined to find the Osiris Code now that they know we have the first fragment."

Vohowa nodded, her eyes filled with determination. "We need to gather more information about their operations," she said. "We need to know where they are conducting their experiments and what their next moves are."

Orenus listened intently, his mind racing with ideas. He knew that the Seekers had to act quickly and strategically to protect the Osiris Code. "What can we do to stay ahead of them?" he asked, his voice filled with resolve.

Alledas pulled out a map and spread it on the table. The map showed various locations around the world, marked with symbols and notes. "We need to find the next fragment of the Osiris Code before they do," she said. "We have some leads on where the next fragment might be hidden, but we need to act quickly."

Vohowa pulled out her high-tech tablet and started to show Orenus and Alledas the data she had gathered. "I have been tracking their communications and movements," she explained. "They have been focusing their efforts on a few key locations. We need to investigate these locations and find the next fragment before they do."

Alledas nodded in agreement. "We will split into teams," she said. "Vohowa, you will continue to gather information and track their movements. Orenus and I will investigate the key locations and search for the next fragment."

With their plan in place, the Seekers knew that the journey ahead would be long and dangerous, but they were determined to see it through to the end. They were ready to face whatever challenges lay ahead, knowing that they had each other's support and guidance.

Chapter 5: The Ancient Library

New Clue

After the intense encounter with the Ankh Society, Orenus, Alledas, and Vohowa knew they had to act quickly. They regrouped in the Seekers' headquarters, hidden beneath the bustling streets of Cairo. The air was filled with a mix of tension and excitement as they prepared for their next move.

Orenus sat at the large, round table in the mission room, the glowing tablet with the first fragment of the Osiris Code in front of him. He had been studying the tablet for hours, trying to decipher more of its secrets. The symbols and hieroglyphs seemed to dance before his eyes, whispering ancient secrets.

Suddenly, Orenus noticed a pattern in the symbols that he hadn't seen before. His heart started to race as he realized that he might have found a new clue. He quickly pulled out his notebook and started to write down the pattern, comparing it with the notes he had taken earlier.

As he worked, Orenus felt a sense of awe and wonder. He knew that he was standing on the brink of an incredible discovery, one that could change the course of history. He was determined to uncover the secrets of the Osiris Code and protect it from those who would use it for harm.

After what felt like hours, Orenus finally managed to decipher the entire pattern. He looked at the message he had written down and felt a shiver run down his spine. The message talked about an ancient library hidden deep in the desert, where the next fragment of the Osiris Code was hidden.

Orenus knew that he had to share this new clue with the Seekers. He quickly gathered his notes and made his way to the mission room, where Alledas and Vohowa were waiting for him.

"I found something," Orenus said, his voice filled with excitement and urgency. "I deciphered more of the tablet, and I found a clue leading to an ancient library hidden in the desert. The next fragment of the Osiris Code is hidden there."

Alledas and Vohowa looked at Orenus with a mix of surprise and pride. They knew that he had made an incredible discovery, one that could bring them one step closer to uncovering the secrets of the Osiris Code.

"This is amazing, Orenus," Alledas said, her voice filled with admiration. "You have done well. This new clue could be the key to finding the next fragment of the Osiris Code."

Vohowa nodded in agreement, her eyes sparkling with excitement. "We need to act quickly," she said. "The Ankh Society will not give up easily, and they will be after the same fragment. We need to stay one step ahead of them."

Alledas looked at Orenus and Vohowa with determination. "We will prepare for our journey to the ancient library," she said. "We will gather our equipment and plan our route through the desert. Together, we will find the next fragment of the Osiris Code and protect it from those who would use it for harm."

Preparing for the Journey

With the new clue in hand, the Seekers knew they had to act quickly. The ancient library hidden in the desert held the next fragment of the Osiris Code, and they couldn't let the Ankh Society get their hands on it.

Alledas spread out a large map of the desert on the table. The map was filled with symbols and notes, marking the locations of ancient temples, hidden oases, and dangerous terrain. "We need to plan our route carefully," she said. "The desert is treacherous, and we need to be prepared for any obstacles we might encounter."

Vohowa pulled out her high-tech tablet and started to input coordinates and data. "I'll use our advanced technology to map out the safest and most efficient route," she said. "We'll need to avoid areas with high concentrations of sandstorms and other natural hazards."

Orenus looked at the map, his mind racing with excitement and a touch of nervousness. He knew that the journey ahead would be challenging, but he was ready to face whatever came their way. "What kind of supplies do we need?" he asked, his voice filled with determination.

Alledas looked at Orenus with a serious expression. "We'll need plenty of water and food," she said. "The desert is unforgiving, and we need to stay hydrated and nourished. We'll also need protective gear to shield us from the sun and sand."

Vohowa nodded in agreement. "We'll need advanced navigation tools and communication devices," she added. "We need to stay in contact with each other and with the headquarters in case of any emergencies."

Orenus listened intently, taking mental notes of everything they would need. He knew that the success of their mission depended on thorough preparation and careful planning. "What about ancient magic and technology?" he asked. "Will we need any special tools or artifacts?"

Alledas smiled, her eyes filled with pride. "Yes, we will," she said. "We'll need to bring ancient artifacts that can help us navigate the hidden temples and uncover the secrets of the Osiris Code. We'll also need advanced technology to decipher the code and stay ahead of the Ankh Society."

Vohowa pulled out a small device from her pocket and showed it to Orenus. "This is a high-tech scanner," she explained. "It can detect hidden artifacts and symbols, and it will be crucial for our mission. We'll also bring some ancient scrolls and texts that contain valuable information about the Osiris Code."

As the Seekers gathered their supplies and planned their route, the atmosphere in the headquarters was filled with a mix of excitement and tension. They knew that the journey ahead would be long and dangerous, but they were determined to see it through to the end.

Alledas, Vohowa, and Orenus worked together, packing their bags with water, food, protective gear, and advanced technology. They double-checked their equipment, making sure everything was in working order and ready for the journey.

Finally, after hours of preparation, the Seekers were ready to embark on their mission. Alledas looked at Orenus and Vohowa with determination. "We have everything we need," she said. "Now, let's go find the next fragment of the Osiris Code and protect it from those who would use it for harm."

Orenus felt a surge of adrenaline rush through his body. He knew that this was the moment they had been preparing for, the moment when they would face the challenges of the desert and uncover the secrets of the Osiris Code. He was ready to do whatever it took to protect the code and ensure it was used for good.

Vohowa smiled, her eyes filled with excitement and anticipation. "Let's do this," she said. "Together, we will achieve great things. We will uncover the secrets of the Osiris Code and bring balance to the world."

With their bags packed and their route planned, the Seekers set off on their journey to the ancient library hidden in the desert. They knew that the road ahead would be filled with danger and excitement, but they were determined to see it through to the end. Together, they would protect the Osiris Code and bring balance to the world.

The Desert Journey

The sun was high in the sky, casting a relentless heat over the vast expanse of the desert. Orenus, Alledas, and Vohowa set off on their journey, their bags filled with supplies and their hearts filled with determination. The desert stretched out before them, a seemingly endless sea of sand and rock.

Alledas led the way, using a combination of ancient magic and advanced technology to navigate the treacherous terrain. She held a small, glowing orb in her hand, which seemed to guide them through the desert. "This orb is enchanted with ancient magic," she explained. "It will help us find the safest path to the ancient library."

Vohowa walked beside Alledas, her high-tech tablet in hand. She used the tablet to scan the horizon, looking for any signs of danger or hidden traps. "The desert is filled with ancient magic and hidden dangers," she said. "We need to stay alert and be prepared for anything."

Orenus followed closely behind, his eyes scanning the landscape for any clues or signs that could help them on their journey. He felt a mix of excitement and nervousness, knowing that the road ahead would be filled with challenges and surprises.

As they walked, the sun beat down on them, and the sand shifted beneath their feet. The desert was unforgiving, but the Seekers were determined to press on. They took frequent breaks to drink water and rest, making sure to conserve their energy for the journey ahead.

Suddenly, a strong wind began to blow, kicking up sand and dust. The sky darkened, and the air grew thick with the sound of howling wind. Orenus looked up, his heart pounding with fear. "Is that a sandstorm?" he asked, his voice barely audible over the roar of the wind.

Alledas nodded, her eyes filled with concern. "Yes, it is," she said. "We need to find shelter quickly. Sandstorms can be deadly in the desert."

Vohowa quickly pulled out her tablet and started scanning the area for any signs of shelter. "There's a small cave nearby," she said, pointing in the direction of a rocky outcrop. "We need to get there as fast as we can."

The Seekers hurried towards the cave, battling against the wind and sand. The storm grew stronger with each passing moment, making it difficult to see and breathe. Orenus felt a sense of panic rising within him, but he pushed it down, focusing on the task at hand.

Finally, after what felt like an eternity, they reached the cave. They quickly ducked inside, seeking refuge from the raging storm. The cave was small and dark, but it provided the shelter they needed.

Alledas pulled out a small, glowing crystal from her bag and placed it in the center of the cave. The crystal emitted a soft, warm light, filling the space with a comforting glow. "This crystal is enchanted with ancient magic," she explained. "It will protect us from the sandstorm and keep us safe until the storm passes."

The Seekers huddled together in the cave, waiting for the sandstorm to pass. They shared stories and plans, their voices filled with determination and hope. They knew that the journey ahead would be long and dangerous, but they were ready to face whatever challenges lay ahead.

After what felt like hours, the storm finally began to subside. The wind died down, and the sand settled, revealing the vast expanse of the desert once more. The Seekers emerged from the cave, their eyes scanning the horizon for any signs of danger.

As they continued their journey, they encountered more challenges and obstacles. The desert was filled with ancient traps and hidden dangers, but the Seekers were prepared. They used their advanced technology and ancient magic to navigate the treacherous terrain, avoiding the traps and overcoming the obstacles.

At one point, they came across a large, hidden pit filled with sharp spikes. Vohowa quickly used her tablet to scan the area, revealing the trap before it was too late. "This is an ancient trap," she explained. "It was designed to protect the ancient library from intruders. We need to be careful and avoid it."

Alledas nodded in agreement. "We will use our ancient magic to create a safe path around the trap," she said. She pulled out a small, glowing amulet from her bag and held it up, chanting ancient words under her breath. The amulet glowed brighter, and a path of light appeared before them, guiding them safely around the trap.

Orenus felt a sense of awe and wonder at the power of ancient magic and advanced technology. He knew that he was standing on the brink of an incredible adventure, one that could change the course of history.

As the sun began to set, casting a warm glow over the desert, the Seekers knew that they were one step closer to their destination. The ancient library was within reach, and they were determined to find the next fragment of the Osiris Code and protect it from those who would use it for harm.

Arrival at the Library

The sun was beginning to set, casting a warm, golden glow over the vast expanse of the desert. The Seekers had been walking for what felt like an eternity, their bodies tired and their spirits weary. But as they crested a tall dune, they finally saw it: the ancient library, hidden deep within the heart of the desert.

The library was a magnificent structure, built from ancient stone and adorned with intricate carvings and hieroglyphs. It stood tall and proud, a testament to the wisdom and knowledge of the ancient Egyptians. The Seekers approached the library with a mix of awe and trepidation, knowing that within its walls lay the next fragment of the Osiris Code.

Alledas led the way, her eyes scanning the entrance for any signs of traps or hidden dangers. She held up her glowing orb, which seemed to guide them safely through the ancient doors. "We need to be careful," she said, her voice filled with caution. "The library is filled with ancient magic and secrets. We must tread lightly."

Vohowa followed closely behind, her high-tech tablet in hand. She used the tablet to scan the walls and floors, looking for any hidden symbols or clues that could help them on their journey. "The library is filled with ancient knowledge," she said. "We need to be respectful and mindful of its secrets."

Orenus walked beside Vohowa, his heart pounding with excitement and anticipation. He knew that they were standing on the brink of an incredible discovery, one that could change the course of history.

As they stepped inside the ancient library, the Seekers were struck by the sense of history and mystery that filled the air. The walls were lined with ancient scrolls and texts, all arranged in a way that seemed both chaotic and orderly at the same time. The air was filled with the scent of old parchment and dust, whispering secrets from the past.

Alledas led the way through the winding corridors, her eyes scanning the shelves for any signs of the Osiris Code. She used her ancient magic to decipher the hieroglyphs and symbols, guiding them deeper into the heart of the library.

Suddenly, Orenus noticed a small, glowing tablet resting on a pedestal in the center of a large, circular room. The tablet was covered in more hieroglyphs and symbols, and it seemed to be the source of the mysterious light that filled the chamber. Orenus approached the tablet cautiously, his heart racing with excitement.

"This is it," he said, his voice filled with awe. "This is the next fragment of the Osiris Code."

Vohowa quickly pulled out her tablet and started to scan the symbols on the glowing tablet. She explained each hieroglyph and its meaning, deciphering the code and revealing its secrets. "The Osiris Code is not just a magical algorithm," she said. "It's a combination of ancient magic and advanced technology. It holds the power of resurrection, but it also has the potential to change the world in ways we can't even imagine."

Alledas nodded in agreement, her eyes filled with determination. "We need to gather all the fragments of the Osiris Code and protect them from those who would use them for harm," she said. "Together, we can uncover the secrets of the code and bring balance to the world."

Orenus felt a sense of purpose and determination.

With the next fragment of the Osiris Code safely in their possession, the Seekers knew that the journey had just begun. There were still many more fragments to find, and the road ahead would be filled with danger and excitement. But they were determined to see it through to the end, to protect the Osiris Code and bring balance to the world.

Chapter 6: The Desert Adventure

Exploring the Library

The ancient library was a labyrinth of knowledge and mystery, filled with winding corridors and towering shelves lined with ancient scrolls and texts. The Seekers moved cautiously through the dimly lit chambers, their footsteps echoing softly against the stone walls. The air was thick with the scent of old parchment and the weight of centuries of secrets.

Alledas led the way, her glowing orb casting a soft, ethereal light that illuminated the intricate carvings and hieroglyphs adorning the walls. She used her ancient magic to decipher the symbols, guiding them deeper into the heart of the library. "We must be careful," she whispered. "The library is protected by magical guardians and ancient traps. We need to stay alert."

Vohowa followed closely behind, her high-tech tablet in hand. She scanned the walls and floors, looking for any hidden symbols or clues that could help them on their journey. "The library is filled with ancient knowledge," she said. "We need to be respectful and mindful of its secrets."

Orenus walked beside Vohowa, his eyes scanning the shelves for any signs of the Osiris Code. He felt a mix of excitement and nervousness, knowing that the road ahead would be filled with challenges and surprises. "What kind of guardians should we expect?" he asked, his voice filled with curiosity.

Alledas looked at Orenus with a serious expression. "The guardians can take many forms," she said. "They could be magical creatures, ancient spirits, or even enchanted artifacts. We need to be prepared for anything."

As they ventured deeper into the library, the Seekers encountered their first challenge. A large, stone statue of a sphinx stood in their path, its eyes glowing with an otherworldly light. The sphinx spoke in a deep, resonating voice, "Who seeks the knowledge of the Osiris Code?"

Orenus stepped forward, his heart pounding with determination. He knew that they had to answer the sphinx's riddle correctly to proceed. "We are the Seekers," he said. "We seek the Osiris Code to protect it from those who would use it for harm."

The sphinx nodded, its eyes narrowing as it studied Orenus. "Very well," it said. "Answer my riddle, and you may pass. Fail, and you will face my wrath. What walks on four legs in the morning, two legs at noon, and three legs in the evening?"

Orenus thought carefully, his mind racing through the possibilities. He remembered the stories he had read about sphinxes and their riddles. Suddenly, it clicked. "A human," he said confidently. "A human crawls on four legs as a baby, walks on two legs as an adult, and uses a cane, which is like a third leg, in old age."

The sphinx nodded, its eyes glowing with approval. "You have answered correctly," it said. "You may pass."

With the sphinx's blessing, the Seekers continued their exploration of the ancient library. They encountered more challenges along the way, including ancient traps and magical guardians. Each time, they used their deep thinking and combined knowledge of ancient magic and advanced technology to overcome the obstacles.

In one chamber, they found a series of pressure plates on the floor, each marked with a different hieroglyph. Vohowa used her tablet to scan the plates, revealing a pattern that needed to be followed to avoid triggering a trap. "We need to step on the plates in the correct order," she said. "If we make a mistake, the trap will be activated."

Alledas studied the pattern carefully, using her ancient magic to decipher the hieroglyphs. "The pattern represents the journey of the sun," she said. "We need to follow the path of the sun from dawn to dusk."

Orenus nodded, his heart filled with determination. He stepped carefully onto the first plate, following the path of the sun as Alledas had described. One by one, the Seekers made their way across the chamber, avoiding the trap and reaching the other side safely.

As they continued their exploration, the Seekers found more fragments of the Osiris Code hidden within the ancient library. Each fragment was guarded by a magical guardian or an ancient trap, but the Seekers used their deep thinking and combined skills to overcome the challenges.

With each fragment they found, the Seekers knew that they were one step closer to uncovering the secrets of the Osiris Code and protecting it from those who would use it for harm. They were determined to see their mission through to the end, no matter what challenges lay ahead.

Overcoming Challenges

As the Seekers ventured deeper into the ancient library, they encountered a series of increasingly complex challenges. Each chamber they entered seemed to be guarded by a new set of traps and magical guardians, all designed to protect the secrets of the Osiris Code.

In one chamber, they found a large, intricate puzzle carved into the stone floor. The puzzle consisted of interlocking symbols and hieroglyphs, each one representing a different aspect of ancient Egyptian mythology. Orenus stepped forward, his eyes scanning the puzzle with a mix of excitement and determination.

"This looks like a combination lock," he said, his voice filled with curiosity. "We need to find the correct sequence of symbols to unlock the next chamber."

Vohowa pulled out her high-tech tablet and started to scan the puzzle, using advanced algorithms to decipher the symbols. "The sequence is based on the journey of the gods," she explained. "We need to follow the path of Osiris, Isis, and Horus to unlock the puzzle."

Alledas nodded in agreement, her eyes filled with pride. "Orenus, you have the hacking skills to decipher this puzzle," she said. "Use your knowledge of ancient magic and technology to find the correct sequence."

Orenus took a deep breath and started to analyze the puzzle. He used his hacking skills to decipher the symbols, comparing them with the notes he had taken earlier. Slowly, he began to piece together the correct sequence, following the path of the gods as Vohowa had described.

After what felt like hours, Orenus finally managed to decipher the entire sequence. He entered the symbols in the correct order, and the puzzle clicked open, revealing a hidden passage leading to the next chamber.

In the next chamber, the Seekers encountered a magical guardian in the form of a giant, winged serpent. The serpent coiled around a pedestal, its eyes glowing with an otherworldly light. On the pedestal rested another fragment of the Osiris Code, glowing with a mysterious light.

Alledas stepped forward, her voice filled with authority. "We come in peace," she said. "We seek the Osiris Code to protect it from those who would use it for harm. We mean no disrespect to the ancient guardians of this library."

The serpent hissed, its eyes narrowing as it studied the Seekers. "You seek the power of the Osiris Code," it said. "But you must prove your worth. Answer my riddle, and you may take the fragment. Fail, and you will face my wrath."

Orenus stepped forward, his heart pounding with determination. He knew that they had to answer the serpent's riddle correctly to proceed. "We are ready to prove our worth," he said.

The serpent nodded; its eyes glowing brighter. "What is so fragile that saying its name breaks it?" it asked.

Orenus thought carefully, his mind racing through the possibilities. He remembered the stories he had read about riddles and their solutions. Suddenly, it clicked. "Silence," he said confidently. "Saying the name 'silence' breaks the silence."

The serpent nodded, its eyes glowing with approval. "You have answered correctly," it said. "You may take the fragment of the Osiris Code."

With the serpent's blessing, the Seekers carefully retrieved the fragment from the pedestal, adding it to their collection. They knew that each fragment they found brought them one step closer to uncovering the secrets of the Osiris Code and protecting it from those who would use it for harm.

As the Seekers continued their exploration of the ancient library, they encountered more challenges and obstacles. Each time, they used their combined skills and knowledge to overcome the obstacles, working together as a team to find more fragments of the Osiris Code.

In one chamber, they found a series of ancient artifacts scattered across the floor. Each artifact was marked with a different hieroglyph, and they seemed to be part of a larger puzzle. Vohowa used her tablet to scan the artifacts, revealing a pattern that needed to be followed to unlock the next fragment of the code.

"We need to arrange the artifacts in the correct order," she said. "The pattern represents the journey of the sun, moon, and stars. We need to follow the path of the celestial bodies to unlock the puzzle."

Orenus nodded, his heart filled with determination. He used his hacking skills to decipher the hieroglyphs, comparing them with the notes he had taken earlier. Slowly, he began to piece together the correct sequence, following the path of the celestial bodies as Vohowa had described.

After what felt like hours, Orenus finally managed to decipher the entire sequence. He arranged the artifacts in the correct order, and the puzzle clicked open, revealing another fragment of the Osiris Code.

With each challenge they overcame, the Seekers grew stronger and more determined. They knew that the journey ahead would be long and dangerous, but they were ready to face whatever challenges lay ahead. Together, they would protect the Osiris Code and bring balance to the world.

As they gathered more fragments of the code, the Seekers knew that they were one step closer to uncovering the secrets of the Osiris Code and protecting it from those who would use it for harm. They were determined to see their mission through to the end, no matter what challenges lay ahead.

The Final Fragment

After overcoming numerous challenges and obstacles, the Seekers found themselves in the heart of the ancient library. The air was thick with anticipation and the weight of centuries of secrets. They knew they were close to their goal; the final fragment of the Osiris Code.

Alledas led the way, her glowing orb casting a soft, ethereal light that illuminated the intricate carvings and hieroglyphs adorning the walls. She used her ancient magic to decipher the symbols, guiding them deeper into the heart of the library. "We are almost there," she whispered, her voice filled with determination.

Vohowa followed closely behind, her high-tech tablet in hand. She scanned the walls and floors, looking for any hidden symbols or clues that could help them on their journey. "The library is filled with ancient knowledge," she said. "We need to be respectful and mindful of its secrets."

Orenus walked beside Vohowa, his eyes scanning the shelves for any signs of the Osiris Code. He felt a mix of excitement and nervousness, knowing that the road ahead would be filled with challenges and surprises. "What do you think the final fragment will look like?" he asked, his voice filled with curiosity.

Alledas looked at Orenus with a serious expression. "The final fragment will be the key to unlocking the full power of the Osiris Code," she said. "It will be heavily guarded and protected by ancient magic and technology. We need to be prepared for anything."

As they ventured deeper into the library, the Seekers encountered a large, ornate chamber filled with ancient artifacts and strange symbols. In the center of the chamber stood a pedestal, upon which rested a glowing tablet. The tablet was covered in intricate hieroglyphs and symbols, and it seemed to be the source of the mysterious light that filled the chamber.

Orenus approached the tablet cautiously, his heart racing with excitement and anticipation. "This is it," he said, his voice filled with awe. "This is the final fragment of the Osiris Code."

Vohowa quickly pulled out her tablet and started to scan the symbols on the glowing tablet. She explained each hieroglyph and its meaning, deciphering the code and revealing its secrets. "The Osiris Code is not just a magical algorithm," she said. "It's a combination of ancient magic and advanced technology. It holds the power of resurrection, but it also has the potential to change the world in ways we can't even imagine."

Alledas nodded in agreement, her eyes filled with determination. "We need to gather all the fragments of the Osiris Code and protect them from those who would use them for harm," she said. "Together, we can uncover the secrets of the code and bring balance to the world."

Suddenly, the chamber began to shake, and the walls started to glow with an otherworldly light. The Seekers looked around in alarm, realizing that they had triggered a hidden trap. "We need to act quickly," Alledas said, her voice filled with urgency. "We need to decipher the final fragment and escape before the trap is activated."

Orenus, Alledas, and Vohowa worked together, using their combined skills and knowledge to decipher the final fragment of the Osiris Code. They used their advanced technology and ancient magic to overcome the challenges posed by the trap, working quickly and efficiently to unlock the secrets of the code.

As they deciphered the final fragment, the Seekers realized the true importance of the Osiris Code and the dangers it posed. They knew that in the wrong hands, the code could be used to control life and death, to gain ultimate power and dominion over the world. They were determined to protect the code and ensure it was used for good.

Finally, after what felt like hours, the Seekers managed to decipher the entire final fragment. They gathered the fragment and made their way out of the chamber, just as the trap was activated. The walls began to close in, and the floor started to shake, but the Seekers used their advanced technology and ancient magic to escape just in time.

As they emerged from the ancient library, the Seekers knew that they had achieved something incredible. They had found the final fragment of the Osiris Code and uncovered its secrets. They were one step closer to protecting the code and bringing balance to the world.

Alledas looked at Orenus and Vohowa with pride and respect. "You have done well today," she said. "Together, we have achieved something incredible. We have found the final fragment of the Osiris Code and uncovered its secrets. Now, we must protect the code and ensure it is used for good."

Orenus felt a sense of purpose and determination.

With the final fragment of the Osiris Code safely in their possession, the Seekers knew that the journey had just begun. There were still many challenges and dangers ahead, but they were determined to see it through to the end, to protect the Osiris Code and bring balance to the world.

Leaving the Library

With the final fragment of the Osiris Code safely in their possession, the Seekers knew that their mission in the ancient library was complete. They had overcome countless challenges and obstacles, using their combined skills and knowledge to decipher the code and protect it from those who would use it for harm.

Alledas led the way out of the library, her glowing orb casting a soft, ethereal light that illuminated the intricate carvings and hieroglyphs adorning the walls. She used her ancient magic to guide them safely through the winding corridors and hidden passages, ensuring that they avoided any remaining traps or guardians.

Vohowa followed closely behind, her high-tech tablet in hand. She scanned the walls and floors, looking for any hidden symbols or clues that could help them on their journey. "We need to be careful," she said. "The library is filled with ancient magic and secrets. We must tread lightly."

Orenus walked beside Vohowa, his eyes scanning the shelves for any signs of danger. He felt a mix of excitement and relief, knowing that they had achieved something incredible. "I can't believe we found the final fragment," he said, his voice filled with awe. "We've come so far."

Alledas looked at Orenus with a serious expression. "Yes, we have," she said. "But our journey is far from over. We need to return to our headquarters and prepare for the next steps. The Ankh Society will not give up easily, and we need to stay one step ahead of them."

As they made their way out of the library, the Seekers encountered one final challenge. A large, stone door blocked their path, adorned with intricate carvings and hieroglyphs. The door was covered in ancient symbols and magical wards, designed to protect the library from intruders.

Alledas stepped forward, her eyes scanning the symbols on the door. She used her ancient magic to decipher the hieroglyphs, looking for any clues that could help them unlock the door. "This door is protected by ancient magic," she said. "We need to find the correct sequence of symbols to unlock it."

Vohowa quickly pulled out her tablet and started to scan the door, using advanced algorithms to decipher the symbols. "The sequence is based on the journey of the gods," she explained. "We need to follow the path of Osiris, Isis, and Horus to unlock the door."

Orenus nodded, his heart filled with determination. He used his hacking skills to decipher the symbols, comparing them with the notes he had taken earlier. Slowly, he began to piece together the correct sequence, following the path of the gods as Vohowa had described.

After what felt like hours, Orenus finally managed to decipher the entire sequence. He entered the symbols in the correct order, and the door clicked open, revealing the vast expanse of the desert beyond.

The Seekers stepped out of the ancient library, their hearts filled with a sense of accomplishment and purpose. They knew that they had achieved something incredible, that they had found the final fragment of the Osiris Code and uncovered its secrets. But they also knew that their journey was far from over.

Alledas looked at Orenus and Vohowa with pride and respect. "You have done well today," she said. "Together, we have achieved something incredible. We have found the final fragment of the Osiris Code and uncovered its secrets. Now, we must return to our headquarters and prepare for the next steps."

Orenus felt a sense of purpose and determination.

With the fragments of the Osiris Code safely in their possession, the Seekers prepared to return to their headquarters.

Chapter 7: The Betrayal

The Return Journey

The journey back to the Seekers' headquarters was filled with a mix of excitement and relief. The desert stretched out before them, a seemingly endless sea of sand and rock, but the Seekers knew they were on the right path. They had accomplished something incredible, finding the final fragment of the Osiris Code and uncovering its secrets.

Alledas led the way, her glowing orb casting a soft, ethereal light that illuminated the path ahead. She used her ancient magic to guide them safely through the treacherous terrain, ensuring that they avoided any hidden dangers or traps.

Vohowa followed closely behind, her high-tech tablet in hand. She scanned the horizon, looking for any signs of danger or pursuit. "We need to stay alert," she said. "The Ankh Society will not give up easily. They will be after the Osiris Code, and we need to be prepared for anything."

Orenus walked beside Vohowa, his eyes scanning the landscape for any signs of trouble. He felt a mix of excitement and nervousness, knowing that the road ahead would be filled with challenges and surprises. "What do you think our next steps should be?" he asked, his voice filled with curiosity.

Alledas looked at Orenus with a serious expression. "We need to gather all the fragments of the Osiris Code and protect them from those who would use them for harm," she said. "We need to decipher the code fully and understand its true power. Only then can we ensure it is used for good."

As they continued their journey, the Seekers discussed their next steps and the importance of the Osiris Code. They knew that the code held the power of resurrection, but it also had the potential to change the world in ways they could not even imagine. They were determined to protect the code and ensure it was used for good.

"The Osiris Code is too powerful to be left unprotected," Alledas said. "In the wrong hands, it could be used to control life and death, to gain ultimate power and dominion over the world. We must be vigilant and prepared for any threat."

Vohowa nodded in agreement, her eyes filled with determination. "We need to use our advanced technology and ancient magic to stay one step ahead of the Ankh Society," she said. "We need to gather information, decipher the code, and navigate the hidden temples before they can."

Orenus felt a sense of purpose and determination.

Finally, after what felt like an eternity, the Seekers reached the hidden entrance to their headquarters. They stepped inside, feeling a sense of accomplishment and relief. They had returned safely, with the fragments of the Osiris Code in their possession.

Alledas looked at Orenus and Vohowa with pride and respect. "You have done well today," she said. "Together, we have achieved something incredible. We have found the final fragment of the Osiris Code and uncovered its secrets. Now, we must prepare for the next steps."

The Betrayal

The Seekers gathered in the mission room, their hearts filled with a sense of accomplishment and purpose. They had returned safely from the ancient library, with the fragments of the Osiris Code in their possession. The air was thick with anticipation as they prepared to discuss their next steps.

Suddenly, the door to the mission room burst open, and a familiar figure stepped inside. It was one of the Seekers, a man named Khepri, who had been with the group for years. But there was something different about him this time—his eyes were filled with a cold, calculating look, and he held a small, glowing device in his hand.

"Khepri, what are you doing?" Alledas asked, her voice filled with concern and confusion.

Khepri looked at Alledas with a smirk. "I'm doing what I should have done a long time ago," he said. "I'm taking the Osiris Code for myself—or rather, for the Ankh Society."

Orenus felt a shiver run down his spine. He knew that the Ankh Society was a serious threat, and that the Osiris Code in their hands could be disastrous. He was determined to stop Khepri and protect the code at all costs.

Alledas stepped forward, her eyes filled with determination. "You will not get away with this, Khepri," she said. "The Osiris Code is too powerful to be left in the wrong hands. We will stop you."

Khepri laughed, his eyes glinting with malice. "You can try," he said. "But you will fail. The Ankh Society has promised me power and wealth beyond my wildest dreams. I will not let you stand in my way."

Orenus knew that they had to act quickly. He looked at Alledas, and they shared a silent understanding. They needed to work together to stop Khepri and protect the Osiris Code.

Alledas used her ancient magic to create a barrier around the mission room, preventing Khepri from escaping. She chanted ancient words under her breath, and the air shimmered with magical energy. "You will not leave this room with the Osiris Code," she said, her voice filled with authority.

Khepri's eyes narrowed, and he activated the glowing device in his hand. The device emitted a bright, blinding light, filling the room with a dazzling display of colors and shapes. The Seekers were momentarily disoriented, giving Khepri the chance he needed to make his move.

Orenus quickly recovered from the disorientation and used his hacking skills to disrupt the device's signal. He pulled out his own high-tech tablet and started to input commands, using advanced algorithms to counteract the device's effects. "We need to disable his device," he said, his voice filled with urgency. "It's the key to his escape."

Alledas nodded, her eyes filled with determination. She used her ancient magic to enhance Orenus's hacking abilities, creating a powerful combination of magic and technology. Together, they worked quickly and efficiently, using their combined skills to disable Khepri's device.

Khepri realized that his plan was failing and tried to make a run for it. He dashed towards the door, but Alledas's magical barrier held strong, preventing him from escaping. He turned to face the Seekers, his eyes filled with desperation and anger.

Orenus and Alledas knew that they had to act quickly to stop Khepri and protect the Osiris Code. They used their combined skills and knowledge to corner Khepri, using ancient magic and advanced technology to subdue him.

Alledas chanted ancient words under her breath, and the air shimmered with magical energy. She created a binding spell, wrapping Khepri in invisible chains that prevented him from moving. "You will not escape with the Osiris Code," she said, her voice filled with authority.

Orenus used his hacking skills to disable Khepri's device completely, ensuring that he could not use it to escape or communicate with the Ankh Society. He looked at Khepri with a mix of anger and disappointment. "You betrayed us," he said. "You betrayed the Seekers and everything we stand for. Why?"

Khepri looked at Orenus with a cold, calculating expression. "Power," he said. "The Ankh Society promised me power and wealth beyond my wildest dreams. I couldn't resist the temptation."

Alledas looked at Khepri with a serious expression. "Your actions have put us all in danger," she said. "The Osiris Code is too powerful to be left in the wrong hands. We will not let you succeed."

With Khepri subdued and the Osiris Code safely in their possession, the Seekers knew that they had overcome a serious threat. But they also knew that the journey ahead would be filled with danger and excitement. They were determined to see it through to the end, to protect the Osiris Code and bring balance to the world.

The Chase

With Khepri subdued but not yet captured, Orenus and Alledas knew they had to act quickly. The traitor had managed to slip away during the commotion, and they couldn't let him get away with the fragments of the Osiris Code. They grabbed their gear and rushed out of the mission room, determined to catch Khepri before he could escape.

The headquarters was a labyrinth of ancient corridors and hidden passages, but Alledas knew every twist and turn. She led the way, her glowing orb casting a soft, ethereal light that illuminated the path ahead. Orenus followed closely behind, his heart pounding with adrenaline and determination.

As they raced through the corridors, they encountered various challenges and obstacles. Khepri had activated ancient traps and magical wards to slow them down, but the Seekers were prepared. Alledas used her ancient magic to decipher the hieroglyphs and symbols, guiding them safely through the traps.

"We need to be careful," Alledas said, her voice filled with urgency. "Khepri knows these corridors as well as we do. He will use every trick he knows to escape."

Orenus nodded, his eyes scanning the walls and floors for any signs of danger. He used his hacking skills to scan the area, looking for any hidden devices or traps that Khepri might have left behind. "We need to stay one step ahead of him," he said. "We can't let him get away with the Osiris Code."

As they continued their chase, the Seekers encountered more challenges and obstacles. In one corridor, they found a series of pressure plates on the floor, each marked with a different hieroglyph. Vohowa, who had joined them in the pursuit, used her tablet to scan the plates, revealing a pattern that needed to be followed to avoid triggering a trap.

"We need to step on the plates in the correct order," she said. "If we make a mistake, the trap will be activated."

Alledas studied the pattern carefully, using her ancient magic to decipher the hieroglyphs. "The pattern represents the journey of the sun," she said. "We need to follow the path of the sun from dawn to dusk."

Orenus nodded, his heart filled with determination. He stepped carefully onto the first plate, following the path of the sun as Alledas had described. One by one, the

Seekers made their way across the corridor, avoiding the trap and reaching the other side safely.

As they continued their pursuit, they encountered more traps and magical guardians. Each time, they used their combined skills and knowledge to overcome the obstacles, working quickly and efficiently to catch up to Khepri.

In one chamber, they found a large, intricate puzzle carved into the stone floor. The puzzle consisted of interlocking symbols and hieroglyphs, each one representing a different aspect of ancient Egyptian mythology. Orenus stepped forward, his eyes scanning the puzzle with a mix of excitement and determination.

"This looks like a combination lock," he said, his voice filled with curiosity. "We need to find the correct sequence of symbols to unlock the next chamber."

Vohowa pulled out her high-tech tablet and started to scan the puzzle, using advanced algorithms to decipher the symbols. "The sequence is based on the journey of the gods," she explained. "We need to follow the path of Osiris, Isis, and Horus to unlock the puzzle."

Alledas nodded in agreement, her eyes filled with pride. "Orenus, you have the hacking skills to decipher this puzzle," she said. "Use your knowledge of ancient magic and technology to find the correct sequence."

Orenus took a deep breath and started to analyze the puzzle. He used his hacking skills to decipher the symbols, comparing them with the notes he had taken earlier. Slowly, he began to piece together the correct sequence, following the path of the gods as Vohowa had described.

After what felt like hours, Orenus finally managed to decipher the entire sequence. He entered the symbols in the correct order, and the puzzle clicked open, revealing a hidden passage leading to the next chamber.

As they made their way through the hidden passage, the Seekers knew that they were one step closer to catching Khepri and protecting the Osiris Code. They could hear the sound of footsteps and voices echoing through the ancient stone corridors, growing louder and closer with each passing moment.

Finally, they caught up to Khepri in a large, open chamber filled with ancient artifacts and strange symbols.

The traitor was cornered, his eyes filled with desperation and anger.

"You will not escape with the Osiris Code," Alledas said, her voice filled with authority. "You have betrayed us and everything we stand for. You will face the consequences of your actions."

Orenus felt a sense of purpose and determination. He knew that they had to stop Khepri and protect the Osiris Code at all costs.

The Escape

The large, open chamber was filled with ancient artifacts and strange symbols, casting an eerie glow over the scene. Khepri, the traitor, was cornered, his eyes filled with desperation and anger. Orenus and Alledas stood before him, their hearts pounding with determination and adrenaline.

"You will not escape with the Osiris Code," Alledas said, her voice filled with authority. "You have betrayed us and everything we stand for. You will face the consequences of your actions."

Khepri's eyes narrowed, and he lunged forward, attempting to push past the Seekers. Orenus reacted quickly, using his newfound magical abilities to create a barrier of energy, blocking Khepri's path. The traitor stumbled back, his face contorted with frustration.

Alledas chanted ancient words under her breath, and the air shimmered with magical energy. She created a binding spell, wrapping Khepri in invisible chains that prevented him from moving. "You will not escape," she said, her voice filled with resolve.

Orenus used his hacking skills to disable any remaining devices Khepri might have, ensuring that he could not communicate with the Ankh Society or activate any more traps. "We need to secure the fragments of the Osiris Code," he said, his voice filled with urgency.

Alledas nodded, her eyes filled with determination. "We need to act quickly. The Ankh Society will be after us, and we need to stay one step ahead of them."

With Khepri subdued, Orenus and Alledas gathered the fragments of the Osiris Code, ensuring they were safely secured. They knew that their mission was far from over, and that the Ankh Society would not give up easily.

As they made their way back through the ancient corridors, they could hear the sound of footsteps and voices echoing through the stone walls. The Ankh Society was closing in, and they needed to escape quickly.

Alledas used her ancient magic to create a diversion, casting a spell that filled the corridors with a dazzling display of lights and sounds. The distraction gave the Seekers the chance they needed to slip away unnoticed.

Orenus and Alledas rushed through the hidden passages and secret doors, using their knowledge of the ancient magic and advanced technology to navigate the treacherous terrain. They could feel the weight of the Osiris Code in their possession, knowing that they had to protect it at all costs.

Finally, they reached the hidden entrance to their headquarters, their hearts pounding with relief and exhaustion. They stepped inside, feeling a sense of accomplishment and purpose. They had escaped with the fragments of the Osiris Code, but they knew that the Ankh Society was now aware of their location.

Alledas looked at Orenus with a serious expression. "We need to prepare for the next steps," she said. "The Ankh Society will not give up easily. They will be after us, and we need to stay one step ahead of them."

Orenus felt a sense of purpose and determination. He knew that the journey ahead would be long and dangerous, but he was ready to face whatever challenges lay ahead. Together, they would protect the Osiris Code and bring balance to the world.

With the fragments of the Osiris Code safely in their possession, the Seekers knew that the road ahead would be filled with danger and excitement.

Chapter 8: The Final Showdown

The Attack

The Seekers' headquarters was usually a place of quiet study and strategic planning, but today, it was filled with the sound of alarms and the echo of hurried footsteps. The Ankh Society had launched a full-scale attack, determined to take the fragments of the Osiris Code by force.

Orenus, Alledas, and Vohowa rushed to the mission room, their hearts pounding with adrenaline and determination. They knew that they had to defend their base at all costs. The fragments of the Osiris Code were too important to fall into the wrong hands.

Alledas quickly activated the headquarters' defensive systems, using a combination of ancient magic and advanced technology to create a barrier around the building. The air shimmered with magical energy, and the walls hummed with the power of ancient wards.

"We need to hold them off until we can find a way to escape with the fragments," Alledas said, her voice filled with urgency. "The Ankh Society will not give up easily. They will use every means necessary to get their hands on the Osiris Code."

Vohowa pulled out her high-tech tablet and started scanning the perimeter, looking for any signs of weakness in their defenses. "We need to be strategic," she said. "We can't let them breach our defenses. We need to use our combined skills and knowledge to hold them off."

Orenus nodded, his heart filled with determination. He knew that they had to act quickly and decisively. He used his hacking skills to access the security systems, enhancing their defenses and setting up traps for the invading forces.

As the Ankh Society's forces closed in, the Seekers prepared for battle. They armed themselves with a combination of ancient artifacts and high-tech weapons, ready to defend their base at all costs.

The first wave of attackers breached the outer defenses, storming into the headquarters with a mix of high-tech weapons and ancient magic. The Seekers met them head-on, using their combined skills and knowledge to fend off the attack.

Alledas used her ancient magic to create powerful barriers and magical wards, deflecting the enemy's attacks and protecting the Seekers. She chanted ancient words under her breath, and the air shimmered with magical energy.

Vohowa used her high-tech tablet to control the defensive systems, activating traps and countermeasures to slow down the enemy's advance. She worked quickly and efficiently, using her advanced technology to enhance the Seekers' defenses.

Orenus used his hacking skills to disrupt the enemy's communications and disable their weapons. He worked feverishly, inputting commands and using advanced algorithms to counteract the enemy's attacks.

The battle raged on, with the Seekers fighting valiantly against the overwhelming forces of the Ankh Society. They knew that they had to hold them off long enough to find a way to escape with the fragments of the Osiris Code.

As the fight intensified, Orenus realized that they needed a plan to escape. He turned to Alledas and Vohowa, his eyes filled with determination. "We need to find a way out of here," he said. "We can't hold them off forever. We need to escape with the fragments and protect the Osiris Code."

Alledas nodded, her eyes filled with resolve. "You're right," she said. "We need to find a way to escape. We can't let the Ankh Society get their hands on the Osiris Code. We need to protect it at all costs."

With the battle raging around them, the Seekers knew that they had to act quickly. They had to find a way to escape with the fragments of the Osiris Code and protect it from those who would use it for harm. The road ahead would be filled with danger and excitement, but they were determined to see it through to the end.

The Battle

The battle for the Seekers' headquarters raged on, with the Ankh Society's forces pressing in from all sides. The air was thick with the sound of clashing weapons, the hum of ancient magic, and the desperate cries of combatants. Orenus, Alledas, and Vohowa stood at the heart of the conflict, their hearts pounding with adrenaline and determination.

Alledas used her ancient magic to create powerful barriers and magical wards, deflecting the enemy's attacks and protecting the Seekers. She chanted ancient words under her breath, and the air shimmered with magical energy. Her eyes were filled with resolve as she fought to keep the Ankh Society at bay.

Vohowa used her high-tech tablet to control the defensive systems, activating traps and countermeasures to slow down the enemy's advance. She worked quickly and efficiently, using her advanced technology to enhance the Seekers' defenses. Her eyes scanned the battlefield, looking for any signs of weakness in the enemy's ranks.

Orenus used his hacking skills to disrupt the enemy's communications and disable their weapons. He worked feverishly, inputting commands and using advanced algorithms to counteract the enemy's attacks. His eyes were fixed on his tablet, his fingers dancing over the screen as he fought to turn the tide of the battle.

As the battle intensified, Orenus realized that they needed to use the power of the fragments to gain an advantage. He turned to Alledas and Vohowa, his eyes filled with determination. "We need to use the fragments of the

Osiris Code," he said. "They hold ancient magic that can help us turn the tide of the battle."

Alledas nodded, her eyes filled with resolve. "You're right," she said. "We need to harness the power of the fragments. Together, we can use their magic to defend our base and protect the Osiris Code."

With a newfound determination, the Seekers gathered the fragments of the Osiris Code and began to channel their power. Alledas used her ancient magic to amplify the fragments' energy, creating a powerful barrier around the headquarters that repelled the enemy's attacks.

Vohowa used her high-tech tablet to enhance the fragments' magical properties, integrating them with the headquarters' defensive systems. The air hummed with the combined power of ancient magic and advanced technology, creating a formidable defense against the Ankh Society's forces.

Orenus used his hacking skills to disrupt the enemy's communications and disable their weapons, while also channeling the fragments' power to create magical traps and countermeasures. He worked quickly and efficiently, using his combined skills to turn the tide of the battle.

As the battle raged on, the Seekers fought valiantly against the overwhelming forces of the Ankh Society. They used their combined skills and the power of the fragments to defend their base and protect the Osiris Code. The air was thick with the sound of clashing weapons, the hum of ancient magic, and the desperate cries of combatants.

Suddenly, a group of Ankh Society soldiers breached the outer defenses, storming into the headquarters with a mix of high-tech weapons and ancient magic. The Seekers met them head-on, using their combined skills and knowledge to fend off the attack.

Alledas used her ancient magic to create powerful barriers and magical wards, deflecting the enemy's attacks and protecting the Seekers. She chanted ancient words under her breath, and the air shimmered with magical energy.

Vohowa used her high-tech tablet to control the defensive systems, activating traps and countermeasures to slow down the enemy's advance. She worked quickly and efficiently, using her advanced technology to enhance the Seekers' defenses.

Orenus used his hacking skills to disrupt the enemy's communications and disable their weapons. He worked feverishly, inputting commands and using advanced algorithms to counteract the enemy's attacks. His eyes were fixed on his tablet, his fingers dancing over the screen as he fought to turn the tide of the battle.

The Victory

The battle for the Seekers' headquarters reached its climax. The air was thick with the sound of clashing weapons, the hum of ancient magic, and the desperate cries of combatants. Orenus, Alledas, and Vohowa fought valiantly, using their combined skills and the power of the fragments of the Osiris Code to defend their base.

Alledas chanted ancient words under her breath, amplifying the fragments' energy to create a powerful barrier around the headquarters. The air shimmered with magical energy, deflecting the enemy's attacks and protecting the Seekers. Her eyes were filled with resolve as she fought to keep the Ankh Society at bay.

Vohowa used her high-tech tablet to enhance the fragments' magical properties, integrating them with the headquarters' defensive systems. The air hummed with the combined power of ancient magic and advanced technology, creating a formidable defense against the

Ankh Society's forces. She worked quickly and efficiently, using her advanced technology to enhance the Seekers' defenses.

Orenus used his hacking skills to disrupt the enemy's communications and disable their weapons. He worked feverishly, inputting commands and using advanced algorithms to counteract the enemy's attacks. His eyes were fixed on his tablet, his fingers dancing over the screen as he fought to turn the tide of the battle.

As the battle raged on, the Seekers began to gain the upper hand. Their combined skills and the power of the fragments allowed them to defend their base and protect the Osiris Code. The Ankh Society's forces started to falter, their attacks becoming less coordinated and more desperate.

Suddenly, a group of Ankh Society soldiers breached the outer defenses, storming into the headquarters with a mix of high-tech weapons and ancient magic. The Seekers met them head-on, using their combined skills and knowledge to fend off the attack.

Alledas used her ancient magic to create powerful barriers and magical wards, deflecting the enemy's attacks and protecting the Seekers. She chanted ancient words under her breath, and the air shimmered with magical energy.

Vohowa used her high-tech tablet to control the defensive systems, activating traps and countermeasures to slow down the enemy's advance. She worked quickly and efficiently, using her advanced technology to enhance the Seekers' defenses.

Orenus used his hacking skills to disrupt the enemy's communications and disable their weapons. He worked feverishly, inputting commands and using advanced algorithms to counteract the enemy's attacks. His eyes were fixed on his tablet, his fingers dancing over the screen as he fought to turn the tide of the battle.

As the battle intensified, Orenus realized that they needed to use the power of the fragments to gain a decisive advantage. He turned to Alledas and Vohowa, his eyes filled with determination. "We need to use the fragments of the Osiris Code," he said. "They hold ancient magic that can help us turn the tide of the battle."

Alledas nodded, her eyes filled with resolve. "You're right," she said. "We need to harness the power of the fragments. Together, we can use their magic to defeat the Ankh Society and protect the Osiris Code."

With a newfound determination, the Seekers gathered the fragments of the Osiris Code and began to channel their power. Alledas used her ancient magic to amplify the fragments' energy, creating a powerful barrier around the headquarters that repelled the enemy's attacks.

Vohowa used her high-tech tablet to enhance the fragments' magical properties, integrating them with the headquarters' defensive systems. The air hummed with the combined power of ancient magic and advanced technology, creating a formidable defense against the Ankh Society's forces.

Orenus used his hacking skills to disrupt the enemy's communications and disable their weapons, while also channeling the fragments' power to create magical traps and countermeasures. He worked quickly and efficiently, using his combined skills to turn the tide of the battle.

As the battle raged on, the Seekers fought valiantly against the overwhelming forces of the Ankh Society. They used their combined skills and the power of the fragments to defend their base and protect the Osiris Code. The air was thick with the sound of clashing weapons, the hum of ancient magic, and the desperate cries of combatants.

Suddenly, a group of Ankh Society soldiers breached the outer defenses, storming into the headquarters with a mix of high-tech weapons and ancient magic. The Seekers met them head-on, using their combined skills and knowledge to fend off the attack.

Alledas used her ancient magic to create powerful barriers and magical wards, deflecting the enemy's attacks and protecting the Seekers. She chanted ancient words under her breath, and the air shimmered with magical energy.

Vohowa used her high-tech tablet to control the defensive systems, activating traps and countermeasures to slow down the enemy's advance. She worked quickly and efficiently, using her advanced technology to enhance the Seekers' defenses.

Orenus used his hacking skills to disrupt the enemy's communications and disable their weapons. He worked feverishly, inputting commands and using advanced algorithms to counteract the enemy's attacks. His eyes were fixed on his tablet, his fingers dancing over the screen as he fought to turn the tide of the battle.

As the battle reached its climax, the Seekers began to gain the upper hand. Their combined skills and the power of the fragments allowed them to defend their base and protect the Osiris Code. The Ankh Society's forces started to falter, their attacks becoming less coordinated and more desperate.

Alledas used her ancient magic to create a final, powerful barrier that repelled the enemy's attacks and protected the Seekers. She chanted ancient words under her breath, and the air shimmered with magical energy. The barrier held strong, deflecting the enemy's attacks and protecting the Seekers.

Vohowa used her high-tech tablet to enhance the fragments' magical properties, integrating them with the headquarters' defensive systems. The air hummed with the combined power of ancient magic and advanced technology, creating a formidable defense against the Ankh Society's forces. She worked quickly and efficiently, using her advanced technology to enhance the Seekers' defenses.

Orenus used his hacking skills to disrupt the enemy's communications and disable their weapons. He worked feverishly, inputting commands and using advanced algorithms to counteract the enemy's attacks. His eyes were fixed on his tablet, his fingers dancing over the screen as he fought to turn the tide of the battle.

Finally, the Ankh Society's forces began to retreat, their attacks becoming less coordinated and more desperate. The Seekers had won the battle, defeating the Ankh Society and securing the fragments of the Osiris Code.

Alledas looked at Orenus and Vohowa with pride and respect. "You have done well today," she said. "Together, we have achieved something incredible. We have defeated the Ankh Society and protected the Osiris Code."

Orenus felt a sense of purpose and determination. He knew that they had made the right decision to join the Seekers, that together, they could make a difference.

Vohowa nodded, her eyes filled with resolve. "We have won this battle," she said. "But we must remain vigilant. The Ankh Society will not give up easily. They will regroup and come after us again. We must be prepared for whatever comes next."

Alledas nodded in agreement. "You're right," she said. "We must stay one step ahead of the Ankh Society. We must protect the Osiris Code and ensure it is used for good."

The Aftermath

The battle was over, and the Seekers' headquarters was filled with a mix of relief and exhaustion. The air was thick with the scent of ancient magic and the hum of advanced technology, a testament to the fierce battle that had just taken place. Orenus, Alledas, and Vohowa gathered in the mission room, their hearts heavy with the weight of their victory and the challenges that lay ahead.

Alledas looked at her fellow Seekers with a mix of pride and concern. "We have won a great victory today," she said. "But we must not forget that the journey is far from over. The Ankh Society will not give up easily. They will regroup and come after us again."

Vohowa nodded, her eyes filled with determination. "We need to be prepared for whatever comes next," she said. "We need to stay one step ahead of the Ankh Society and protect the Osiris Code at all costs."

Orenus felt a sense of purpose and determination. He knew that they had made the right decision to join the Seekers, that together, they could make a difference. "What are our next steps?" he asked, his voice filled with curiosity and resolve.

Alledas took a deep breath, her eyes scanning the mission room as she considered their options. "We need to regroup and gather our strength," she said. "We need to analyze the fragments of the Osiris Code and understand their true power. Only then can we decide our next course of action."

Vohowa pulled out her high-tech tablet and started to input commands, using advanced algorithms to analyze the fragments. "The Osiris Code is too powerful to be left unprotected," she said. "We need to decipher its secrets and ensure it is used for good."

Orenus nodded, his heart filled with determination. "We need to find the remaining pieces of the Osiris Code," he said. "We need to protect them from those who would use them for harm. The journey ahead will be long and dangerous, but we must see it through to the end."

Alledas looked at Orenus and Vohowa with pride and respect. "You have both shown great courage and skill," she said. "Together, we can overcome any challenge that comes our way. We must stay united and focused on our mission."

Vohowa nodded, her eyes filled with resolve. "We need to use our combined skills and knowledge to stay one step ahead of the Ankh Society," she said. "We need to be strategic and prepared for whatever comes next."

Orenus felt a sense of purpose and determination. He knew that the journey ahead would be filled with danger and excitement, but he was ready to face whatever challenges lay ahead. "We need to protect the Osiris Code and bring balance to the world," he said. "Together, we can make a difference."

Alledas nodded in agreement. "You're right," she said. "We must stay vigilant and prepared for whatever comes next. The Ankh Society will not give up easily, but together, we can overcome any obstacle."

With the fragments of the Osiris Code safely in their possession, the Seekers knew that the journey had just begun. There were still many challenges and dangers ahead, but they were determined to see it through to the end, to protect the Osiris Code and bring balance to the world.

As they regrouped and discussed their next steps, the Seekers knew that they had to stay united and focused on their mission. They had won a great victory, but the road ahead was long and filled with uncertainty. They had to be prepared for whatever came next, to protect the Osiris Code and ensure it was used for good.

Chapter 9: The Decision

Reflection

In the quiet of his room, Orenus sat alone, his thoughts a whirlwind of memories and emotions. The battle for the Seekers' headquarters was over, but the echoes of the conflict still resonated within him. He held the fragments of the Osiris Code in his hands, their ancient magic humming softly, a reminder of the journey he had undertaken and the importance of the mission ahead.

He looked at the fragments, each one a piece of a puzzle that held the power to change the world. The Osiris Code was not just an ancient artifact; it was a key to unlocking secrets that could bring balance or chaos, depending on who wielded its power. Orenus knew that the responsibility of protecting the code was immense, and it weighed heavily on his shoulders.

His mind drifted back to the moment he first encountered Alledas and the Seekers. He had been a hacker, living on the fringes of society, using his skills to navigate the digital world. But his life had changed forever when he was drawn into the quest for the Osiris Code. He had discovered a world of ancient magic and hidden secrets, a world where the fate of humanity hung in the balance.

Orenus thought about the challenges he had faced and the friends he had made along the way. Alledas, with her ancient wisdom and unwavering determination. Vohowa, with her advanced technology and strategic mind. Together, they had formed a bond that transcended their individual strengths, a bond that had allowed them to overcome seemingly insurmountable obstacles.

He remembered the battles they had fought, the traps they had overcome, and the betrayals they had endured. Each experience had shaped him, had made him stronger and more resolute. He had learned the value of trust, the power of unity, and the importance of their mission.

As Orenus reflected on his journey, he realized that his life had changed forever. He was no longer just a hacker; he was a Seeker, a guardian of ancient secrets and a protector of the Osiris Code. The weight of this responsibility was immense, but it also filled him with a sense of purpose and determination.

He thought about the Ankh Society and the threat they posed. They would not give up easily, and the journey to find the remaining pieces of the Osiris Code would be long and dangerous. But Orenus knew that he was ready to face whatever challenges lay ahead. He had the support and guidance of the Seekers, and together, they could overcome any obstacle.

Orenus looked at the fragments of the Osiris Code once more, their ancient magic pulsing with a quiet power. He knew that the journey ahead would be filled with danger and excitement, but he was ready to see it through to the end. He was ready to protect the Osiris Code and bring balance to the world.

With a newfound determination, Orenus stood up, his heart filled with resolve. He knew that the road ahead would be long and filled with uncertainty, but he was ready to face whatever came next. He was a Seeker, and he would not falter in his mission.

As he stepped out of his room, Orenus knew that he had made the right decision. He had chosen to join the Seekers, to protect the Osiris Code, and to bring balance to the world. And he was ready to see it through to the end, no matter what challenges lay ahead.

The Importance of the Code

Orenus made his way to the mission room, where Alledas and Vohowa were already gathered. The room was filled with a sense of urgency and purpose, a reflection of the challenges they had faced and the importance of their mission. The fragments of the Osiris Code were laid out on the table, their ancient magic pulsing softly, a reminder of the power they held.

Alledas looked up as Orenus entered, her eyes filled with a mix of pride and concern. "Orenus," she said, her voice steady and calm. "We need to discuss the importance of the Osiris Code and the dangers it poses."

Orenus nodded, taking a seat at the table. He looked at the fragments, their ancient magic humming softly, a testament to the power they held. "I've been thinking about the code," he said. "About its importance and the responsibility we have to protect it."

Vohowa leaned forward, her eyes scanning the fragments with a mix of curiosity and caution. "The Osiris Code is not just an ancient artifact," she said. "It holds the power of resurrection, the ability to control life and death. In the wrong hands, it could be used to gain ultimate power and dominion over the world."

Alledas nodded in agreement. "The code is too powerful to be left unprotected," she said. "We must ensure that it is used for good, that it brings balance to the world rather than chaos."

Orenus felt a sense of purpose and determination. He knew that the journey ahead would be long and dangerous, but he was ready to face whatever challenges lay ahead. "We need to keep the code safe," he said. "We need to protect it from those who would use it for harm."

Alledas looked at Orenus and Vohowa with a serious expression. "The Ankh Society will not give up easily," she said. "They will regroup and come after us again. We must be prepared for whatever comes next."

Vohowa nodded, her eyes filled with resolve. "We need to stay one step ahead of the Ankh Society," she said. "We need to use our combined skills and knowledge to protect the code and ensure it is used for good."

Orenus felt a sense of purpose and determination. He knew that the journey ahead would be filled with danger and excitement, but he was ready to face whatever challenges lay ahead. "What are our next steps?" he asked, his voice filled with curiosity and resolve.

Alledas took a deep breath, her eyes scanning the mission room as she considered their options. "We need to analyze the fragments of the Osiris Code and understand their true power," she said. "Only then can we decide our next course of action."

Vohowa pulled out her high-tech tablet and started to input commands, using advanced algorithms to analyze the fragments. "The code is too powerful to be left unprotected," she said. "We need to decipher its secrets and ensure it is used for good."

Orenus nodded, his heart filled with determination. "We need to find the remaining pieces of the Osiris Code," he said. "We need to protect them from those who would use them for harm. The journey ahead will be long and dangerous, but we must see it through to the end."

Alledas looked at Orenus and Vohowa with pride and respect. "You have both shown great courage and skill," she said. "Together, we can overcome any challenge that comes our way. We must stay united and focused on our mission."

Vohowa nodded, her eyes filled with resolve. "We need to use our combined skills and knowledge to stay one step ahead of the Ankh Society," she said. "We need to be strategic and prepared for whatever comes next."

Orenus felt a sense of purpose and determination. He knew that the journey ahead would be filled with danger and excitement, but he was ready to face whatever challenges lay ahead. "We need to protect the Osiris Code and bring balance to the world," he said. "Together, we can make a difference."

Alledas nodded in agreement. "You're right," she said. "We must stay vigilant and prepared for whatever comes next. The Ankh Society will not give up easily, but together, we can overcome any obstacle."

With the fragments of the Osiris Code safely in their possession, the Seekers knew that the journey had just begun. There were still many challenges and dangers ahead, but they were determined to see it through to the end, to protect the Osiris Code and bring balance to the world.

As they discussed the importance of the code and the dangers it posed, the Seekers knew that they had to stay united and focused on their mission. They had won a great victory, but the road ahead was long and filled with uncertainty. They had to be prepared for whatever came next, to protect the Osiris Code and ensure it was used for good.

The Future

As the Seekers concluded their discussion about the importance of the Osiris Code, Orenus found himself lost in thought. The mission room was quiet, filled only with the soft hum of ancient magic and the distant sound of advanced technology. He looked at the fragments of the Osiris Code, their ancient power pulsing gently, a reminder of the journey that lay ahead.

Orenus thought about the future and the challenges they would face. The search for the remaining pieces of the Osiris Code would be long and dangerous, filled with unknown dangers and hidden enemies. The Ankh Society would not give up easily, and they would need to stay one step ahead of them at all times.

He looked at Alledas and Vohowa, his fellow Seekers, and felt a sense of gratitude and camaraderie. They had become more than just allies; they were friends, bound together by their shared mission and the trials they had faced. Together, they had overcome seemingly insurmountable obstacles, and Orenus knew that they could face whatever lay ahead.

Alledas noticed Orenus's thoughtful expression and approached him, her eyes filled with understanding. "You're thinking about the future, aren't you?" she asked softly.

Orenus nodded, his gaze still fixed on the fragments. "Yes," he said. "I'm thinking about the journey ahead and the challenges we'll face. The search for the remaining pieces of the Osiris Code won't be easy."

Alledas placed a reassuring hand on his shoulder. "You're right," she said. "The road ahead will be filled with danger and uncertainty. But remember, we have faced challenges before and emerged stronger. Together, we can overcome anything."

Vohowa joined them, her eyes filled with determination. "We have the power of ancient magic and advanced technology on our side," she said. "With our combined skills and knowledge, we can stay one step ahead of the Ankh Society and protect the Osiris Code."

Orenus felt a surge of resolve. He knew that the journey ahead would be challenging, but he was ready to face whatever came their way. "We need to be strategic," he said. "We need to plan our next steps carefully and be prepared for any eventuality."

Alledas nodded in agreement. "Exactly," she said. "We need to analyze the fragments we have and understand their true power. Only then can we decide our next course of action."

Vohowa pulled out her high-tech tablet and started to input commands, using advanced algorithms to analyze the fragments. "The Osiris Code is too powerful to be left unprotected," she said. "We need to decipher its secrets and ensure it is used for good."

Orenus looked at the fragments, his mind racing with thoughts of the future. He knew that the journey ahead would be long and dangerous, but he was ready to see it through to the end. "We need to find the remaining pieces of the Osiris Code," he said. "We need to protect them from those who would use them for harm. The journey ahead will be challenging, but we must see it through to the end."

Alledas looked at Orenus and Vohowa with pride and respect. "You have both shown great courage and skill," she said. "Together, we can overcome any challenge that comes our way. We must stay united and focused on our mission."

Orenus felt a sense of purpose and determination. He knew that the journey ahead would be filled with danger and excitement, but he was ready to face whatever challenges lay ahead. "We need to protect the Osiris Code and bring balance to the world," he said. "Together, we can make a difference."

Alledas nodded in agreement. "You're right," she said. "We must stay vigilant and prepared for whatever comes next. The Ankh Society will not give up easily, but together, we can overcome any obstacle."

With the fragments of the Osiris Code safely in their possession, the Seekers knew that the journey had just begun. There were still many challenges and dangers ahead, but they were determined to see it through to the end, to protect the Osiris Code and bring balance to the world.

As they discussed the future and the journey ahead, the Seekers knew that they had to stay united and focused on their mission. They had won a great victory, but the road ahead was long and filled with uncertainty. They had to be prepared for whatever came next, to protect the Osiris Code and ensure it was used for good.

With a newfound determination, the Seekers prepared to face the challenges that lay ahead. They knew that the journey would be long and dangerous, but they were ready to see it through to the end, to protect the Osiris Code and bring balance to the world.

Orenus looked at his fellow Seekers, his heart filled with resolve. "We have a long road ahead," he said. "But together, we can overcome any challenge. Let's make sure the Osiris Code is used for good and bring balance to the world."

Alledas and Vohowa nodded in agreement, their eyes filled with determination. Together, they stood ready to face the future, united in their mission to protect the Osiris Code and bring balance to the world.

The Decision

In the quiet of the mission room, Orenus stood before Alledas and Vohowa, his heart filled with a mix of determination and resolve. The fragments of the Osiris Code lay on the table, their ancient magic pulsing softly, a reminder of the journey that lay ahead.

Orenus looked at his fellow Seekers, his eyes filled with a newfound purpose. "I've made my decision," he said, his voice steady and clear. "I will continue this quest with you. I will help find the remaining pieces of the Osiris Code and ensure it is used for good."

Alledas looked at Orenus with pride and respect. "You have shown great courage and skill, Orenus," she said. "Together, we can overcome any challenge that comes our way. We are grateful to have you with us on this journey."

Vohowa nodded in agreement, her eyes filled with determination. "With your hacking skills and magical abilities, you are an invaluable member of our team," she said. "Together, we can stay one step ahead of the Ankh Society and protect the Osiris Code."

Orenus felt a sense of purpose and determination. He knew that the journey ahead would be long and dangerous, but he was ready to face whatever challenges lay ahead. "The Ankh Society will not give up easily," he said. "But we must be prepared for whatever comes next. We must protect the Osiris Code and bring balance to the world."

Alledas nodded, her eyes filled with resolve. "You're right," she said. "The road ahead will be filled with danger and uncertainty, but together, we can overcome any obstacle. We must stay united and focused on our mission."

Vohowa looked at Orenus and Alledas with determination. "We need to use our combined skills and knowledge to stay one step ahead of the Ankh Society," she said. "We need to be strategic and prepared for whatever comes next."

Orenus felt a sense of purpose and determination. He knew that the journey ahead would be filled with danger and excitement, but he was ready to face whatever challenges lay ahead. "We need to protect the Osiris Code and bring balance to the world," he said. "Together, we can make a difference."

Alledas nodded in agreement. "You're right," she said. "We must stay vigilant and prepared for whatever comes next. The Ankh Society will not give up easily, but together, we can overcome any obstacle."

With the fragments of the Osiris Code safely in their possession, the Seekers knew that the journey had just begun. There were still many challenges and dangers ahead, but they were determined to see it through to the end, to protect the Osiris Code and bring balance to the world.

Orenus looked at his fellow Seekers, his heart filled with resolve. "We have a long road ahead," he said. "But together, we can overcome any challenge. Let's make sure the Osiris Code is used for good and bring balance to the world."

Alledas and Vohowa nodded in agreement, their eyes filled with determination. Together, they stood ready to face the future, united in their mission to protect the Osiris Code and bring balance to the world.

As they prepared to embark on the next phase of their journey, the Seekers knew that they had made the right decision. They were ready to face whatever challenges lay ahead, to protect the Osiris Code and ensure it was used for good. With a newfound determination, they stepped forward, ready to see their mission through to the end.

Epilogue

The Global Race

The discovery of the Osiris Code fragments had set off a global race for the remaining pieces. News of the ancient artifact's power spread like wildfire, capturing the attention of governments, secret societies, and powerful individuals around the world. The Seekers knew that the journey ahead would be long and dangerous, filled with unknown dangers and hidden enemies.

In the mission room, Alledas, Vohowa, and Orenus gathered around the table, their eyes fixed on a world map marked with potential locations of the remaining fragments. The air was thick with a mix of excitement and tension, a reflection of the challenges that lay ahead.

Alledas looked at her fellow Seekers with a serious expression. "The discovery of the Osiris Code has set off a global race," she said. "Everyone wants a piece of its power, and they will stop at nothing to get it."

Vohowa nodded, her eyes scanning the map with a mix of curiosity and caution. "We need to be strategic," she said. "We need to plan our next steps carefully and be prepared for any eventuality."

Orenus felt a sense of purpose and determination. He knew that the journey ahead would be filled with danger and excitement, but he was ready to face whatever challenges lay ahead. "We need to stay one step ahead of our competitors," he said. "We need to use our combined skills and knowledge to find the remaining pieces before anyone else does."

Alledas nodded in agreement. "Exactly," she said. "We need to analyze the fragments we have and understand their true power. Only then can we decide our next course of action."

Vohowa pulled out her high-tech tablet and started to input commands, using advanced algorithms to analyze the fragments. "The Osiris Code is too powerful to be left unprotected," she said. "We need to decipher its secrets and ensure it is used for good."

Orenus looked at the fragments, his mind racing with thoughts of the future. He knew that the journey ahead would be long and dangerous, but he was ready to see it through to the end. "We need to find the remaining pieces of the Osiris Code," he said. "We need to protect them from those who would use them for harm. The journey ahead will be challenging, but we must see it through to the end."

Alledas looked at Orenus and Vohowa with pride and respect. "You have both shown great courage and skill," she said. "Together, we can overcome any challenge that comes our way. We must stay united and focused on our mission."

With the fragments of the Osiris Code safely in their possession, the Seekers knew that the journey had just begun. There were still many challenges and dangers ahead, but they were determined to see it through to the end, to protect the Osiris Code and bring balance to the world.

As they prepared for their next mission, the Seekers knew that they had to stay united and focused on their mission. They had won a great victory, but the road ahead was long and filled with uncertainty. They had to be prepared for whatever came next, to protect the Osiris Code and ensure it was used for good.

New Challenges

The Seekers gathered in the mission room, their eyes fixed on the world map marked with potential locations of the remaining fragments. The air was thick with a mix of excitement and tension, a reflection of the challenges that lay ahead.

Alledas looked at her fellow Seekers with a serious expression. "We need to discuss the new challenges we will face in our quest for the Osiris Code," she said. "The Ankh Society and other factions will be after the code as well. We must be prepared for whatever comes next."

Vohowa nodded, her eyes filled with determination. "We need to use our combined skills and knowledge to stay one step ahead of our competitors," she said. "We need to be strategic and prepared for whatever comes next."

Orenus felt a sense of purpose and determination. He knew that the journey ahead would be filled with danger and excitement, but he was ready to face whatever challenges lay ahead. "We need to protect the Osiris Code and bring balance to the world," he said. "Together, we can make a difference."

Alledas nodded in agreement. "You're right," she said. "We must stay vigilant and prepared for whatever comes next. The Ankh Society will not give up easily, but together, we can overcome any obstacle."

Vohowa looked at Orenus and Alledas with determination. "We need to use our combined skills and knowledge to stay one step ahead of the Ankh Society," she said. "We need to be strategic and prepared for whatever comes next."

Orenus felt a sense of purpose and determination. He knew that the journey ahead would be filled with danger and excitement, but he was ready to face whatever challenges lay ahead. "We need to protect the Osiris Code and bring balance to the world," he said. "Together, we can make a difference."

Alledas nodded in agreement. "You're right," she said. "We must stay vigilant and prepared for whatever comes next. The Ankh Society will not give up easily, but together, we can overcome any obstacle."

With the fragments of the Osiris Code safely in their possession, the Seekers knew that the journey had just begun. There were still many challenges and dangers ahead, but they were determined to see it through to the end, to protect the Osiris Code and bring balance to the world.

As they discussed the new challenges they would face, the Seekers knew that they had to stay united and focused on their mission. They had won a great victory, but the road ahead was long and filled with uncertainty. They had to be prepared for whatever came next, to protect the Osiris Code and ensure it was used for good.

The Mysterious Figure

As the Seekers gathered in the mission room, discussing their next steps and the challenges that lay ahead, they were unaware of the eyes that watched them from the shadows. A mysterious figure stood hidden, observing their every move with a mix of curiosity and calculation.

The figure was cloaked in darkness, their features obscured by the dim light. They moved silently, their presence undetected by the Seekers. The figure's eyes were fixed on the fragments of the Osiris Code, a glint of interest and perhaps something more sinister flickering in their gaze.

As the Seekers finalized their plans, the mysterious figure stepped back, melting into the shadows. They knew that the Seekers' journey was far from over, and that new challenges and revelations awaited them. The figure had their own agenda, one that intertwined with the fate of the Osiris Code and the Seekers themselves.

The Seekers, oblivious to the watchful eyes, continued their preparations with determination and resolve. They were ready to face whatever lay ahead, to protect the Osiris Code and bring balance to the world. But the mysterious figure knew that their journey would be filled with unexpected twists and turns, with secrets yet to be uncovered and alliances yet to be forged.

As the Seekers stepped forward, ready to embark on their next mission, the mysterious figure watched from the shadows, a silent witness to the beginning of a new chapter in their quest. The future held many challenges and revelations, and the figure was prepared to play their part in the unfolding drama.

With a final glance at the Seekers, the mysterious figure disappeared into the night, leaving behind a sense of unease and anticipation. The Seekers' journey was far from over, and the future held many surprises, both exciting and dangerous.